SILENT PARTNER

FOX HOLLOW ZODIAC NOVEL 3

MORGAN BRICE

eBook ISBN: 978-1-64795-079-8
Paperback ISBN: 978-1-64795-080-4
Silent Partner, Copyright © 2024 by Gail Z. Martin.
Cover by Adrijus Guscia.

Darkwind Press is an imprint of DreamSpinner Communications, LLC

SILENT PARTNER
FOX HOLLOW ZODIAC NOVEL 3

By Morgan Brice

1

BRANDON

"Hey, Brandon! How did your hike go?"

Brandon Davis looked up at the park ranger's greeting and shook a lock of chestnut hair out of his dark eyes. "Pretty well. We had good weather, no snow, and these folks knew what they were doing. Uneventful."

Ranger Williams chuckled. "Better than the last bunch?"

Brandon rolled his eyes. "Definitely. But that's how it goes. It's their adventure—I'm just the guide."

"I hope you don't have any other long treks planned," the ranger said. "We're about to get some real winter."

"So I heard. I have a few short hikes, nothing major. People who book at this time of year tend to know what they're getting into. Thanks for the heads-up," Brandon replied.

Winter in the northern Adirondacks of New York had a dangerous beauty. Temperatures often fell well below zero. Rocky drop-offs camouflaged by snow could be deadly. Buried trails and markers made it easy for people to lose their way. The forest claimed the unwary, which made Brandon's job as a licensed wilderness guide essential.

"Go get some good food, and for heaven's sake, close your parka! I'm getting frostbite just looking at you," Williams joked.

Brandon jokingly "flashed" Williams, opening the front of his parka wide to display his sweater, henley, and flannel shirt. "I've got layers."

And you're a moose, for fuck's sake, his inner shifter rumbled.

"Go home and have a hot dinner. That's what I plan to do." Williams sent Brandon off with a wave.

"See you next week." Brandon climbed into his ten-year-old Suburban and returned the salute as he drove away.

I hope you're planning on getting vegetables, his moose said. *That awful stuff you take on hikes is not real food.*

You are a very spoiled moose, Brandon jokingly chided his shifter alter-ego. *I buy you the best produce that I can find.*

Let's shift and go strip some branches. Twigs and leaves—yum.

Fortunately for me, I don't have to chew on trees when I'm human.

Your loss.

The last tour had gone well and put a substantial deposit in Brandon's bank account. He had taken four clients on a multi-day outing that included hiking, ice fishing, a pre-set winter camp, and a photo safari to snap pictures of winter wildlife. They were the type of enthusiasts he enjoyed guiding—serious cold-weather outdoors fans who knew what they were doing and were in shape for the adventure.

None of them suspected their guide was also a moose, even as they spotted non-shifter animals in the wild and eagerly snapped photos.

At thirty, Brandon liked his life. He had moved to Fox Hollow, NY, from Plattsburgh, unhappy that his family held their human side in low regard, preferring to stay in their moose form as much as possible. Brandon loved his moose, but he also loved being human. He left as soon as he turned eighteen, already set on making a place for himself in Fox Hollow, a town known as a haven for misfit shifters and psychics.

Now he had his license and certification, as well as first-responder training, and over a decade of experience. Brandon enjoyed meeting people and seeing their awe of the outdoors. While he didn't dare shift on an outing, the strenuous exercise kept him fit, and he liked seeing his clients experience the wonder of the forest. The work was demanding, but he had a base of returning vacationers as well as a steady stream of referrals, enough to buy a cabin not far from Fox Hollow and provide necessities along with occasional comforts.

Working for himself also suited him as an Aries, where he could put his tendencies to be protective, assertive, and a little headstrong to good use.

Brandon's phone rang through the SUV's sound system so he could answer hands-free. "Hey, Drew. What's up?"

"Just making sure you're back and planning on poker night."

"Wouldn't miss it! Everybody else coming?" Brandon smiled at the thought of seeing his friends.

"Yeah, we've got the whole crew. We'll order pizza later. I already shopped for beer and snacks—but I wanted to make sure you've eaten so you don't clean us out," Drew Lowe joked.

"Real funny, Wolfie," Brandon razzed back. "I have to stop for people food since the fridge is empty, but I was planning to strip a few trees before I come over. My other half has *opinions* about trail rations."

"I bet he does," Drew laughed. "I understand. Mine gets snotty if he doesn't get enough steak."

Fox Hollow had a strict "thou shalt not eat thy neighbor" policy, so even though the rest of their usual poker crew were carnivores, Brandon never felt unsafe. Wild wolves were something entirely different.

Brandon's telepathy helped. While he did his best not to intrude on other people's privacy, his ability to read minds made it easier for him to sense threats or insincerity. Years of working with the psychics at the Fox Institute had helped him strengthen his shielding to avoid accidentally rummaging through other people's thoughts, which gave him more confidence to make friends.

"See you after dinner," Drew replied. "Leave a few trees for the rest of us to pee on, okay?"

"No promises. I'm rather peckish," Brandon tossed back.

"I'll tell Russ and the others you'll be here. Hope you don't mind parting with some cash, 'cause I feel lucky."

Brandon snorted. "Keep telling yourself that, dog-boy. Whatever gets you through the night."

"Right back at you, Moose Munch," Drew retorted.

Brandon enjoyed his poker nights. The gang did plenty of razzing and trash-talking, but their joking was never mean, and more than once, they had come together to save lives.

Russ and Drew Lowe, wolf shifter brothers, hosted the weekly game when their commitments to the garage they owned or their EMT duties didn't conflict. Russ's husband Liam Reynard, a fox shifter, ran the local library. Drew's partner, Noah Wilson, was a lynx shifter and nature photographer. Tyler Williams was a bobcat shifter who worked at his family's hotel. Only Justin Miller, the local seaplane pilot, was fully human but he had some helpful psychic abilities.

Brandon felt grateful for a circle of friends who knew the truth about his "other half" and still accepted him. Even more importantly, they weren't afraid of his telepathy, a secret that Brandon shared with few others.

He debated whether to go home and shower or stop at the grocery store on the way. He sniffed the air in the SUV and decided getting cleaned up came first. While people in Fox Hollow were used to people roughing it, even the best deodorant couldn't hold up against several days on the trail.

Once he got home, Brandon pulled the SUV into the garage and unloaded, dividing his gear between what needed to be replenished and what was ready to go again. He ran inside, stripped off his clothes, and ducked under the hot shower, letting it wash away the sweat and dirt of the last several days.

Much as he loved being out in the forest, Brandon was equally happy coming home. The only thing that would make it better would be finding a mate. So far, love had proven elusive.

He rinsed off the soap and toweled, tossed his dirty clothing into the hamper, and dug a new outfit out of his dresser.

He doesn't have to be a moose, Brandon's moose said. *We're not getting any younger. It would just be nice to have someone of our own.*

He dreamed of a partner who could make him laugh, someone enthusiastic about life who liked long chats and lots of cuddling. As an Aries, his ideal match would be a Gemini, but while Brandon took the stars as a guide, he was willing to be open-minded about the details if he met the right guy.

Mixed shifter pairings were common in Fox Hollow, although less so in other places. His friends' marriages proved that. Big vegetarian shifters like deer and elk were rare. He hadn't met another moose shifter since relocating. Brandon believed he could make things work with a carnivore and perhaps even with one of the other omnivore or vegetarian shifters that weren't as large as he was. Brandon was happy for his friends who had found love. And although he was busy with guide tours and being an EMT, he still wished he could find someone special of his own.

Now that he felt suitable to be in public, Brandon drove back to the grocery store. For its size, the shop provided a remarkable variety of products, including some specialties crafted by his neighbors. That saved everyone from trekking to Lake George to go to one of the big-box stores. Online delivery only worked in the summer months.

He parked and headed inside. The familiar mix of smells from the bakery and deli, as well as all the luscious produce, made Brandon sigh happily. He waved to Brenda at the register, grabbed a cart, and started to make the familiar trek around the store.

Brandon loaded up on salad, especially cabbage, broccoli, and cauliflower. He skipped the carrots since they gave him indigestion. That was true for some fruit as well, although he loved frozen berries and added them to the cart. His human side craved coffee, oatmeal, and eggs, so Brandon made sure to replenish. He couldn't resist some chips and cookies and reminded himself to grab a bale of hay from the garden supplies on the store terrace.

Halfway through the store, Brandon stopped dead in his tracks and sniffed the air. A scent he had never picked up before enveloped him, making him light-headed. *Anise and maple. How strange. Maybe they're baking something?*

Mate.

Brandon startled, not expecting to hear from his inner moose in such a human-centric place. *What?*

That's what our mate smells like. Find him!

Brandon seriously doubted he'd spot a moose in the frozen food aisle or even a moose shifter. Still, the scent captivated him and stirred a hunger deep in his groin that had nothing to do with food.

He steered into the next aisle, forcing himself to keep a normal walking pace. *I can't just run past people and sniff them. That would be weird—even for Fox Hollow.*

Shopping forgotten, Brandon searched for the elusive, overwhelming scent. He turned down the baking aisle, and the aroma called to him, far stronger. Only two people were nearby—Mrs. Prendicott—an elderly psychic—and a handsome stranger.

The stranger looked vaguely puzzled like he couldn't find what he wanted on the tightly-packed shelves. The store overstocked during the bad weather months, especially if there was news of a storm in the offing. That sometimes made it difficult to locate items.

Brandon stayed back despite the pull he felt to make the man's acquaintance. The handsome man stood a few inches shorter than Brandon's six-foot-four, with spiked dark blond hair and a defined jawline.

He didn't look like he was from around here. The expensive blue parka was good quality but not hard used, and his insulated boots looked new. His pockets bulged with heavy gloves that peeked from the opening, and a gray scarf wrapped around the man's neck.

Brandon reminded himself not to stare, although between the overwhelming scent and the stranger's good looks, restraining himself took effort.

He did his best to lock down his telepathy, even though everything in him wanted to know more about this man. Brandon permitted himself a superficial sweep, nothing that would dig into secrets or private information, the psychic equivalent of sizing up someone's mood by looking for non-verbal cues.

He's a little off his game in a new place, nervous. Understandable. Worried. Maybe even scared.

Not shifter. Human.

Silent.

To Brandon's surprise, he couldn't read anything else. The man's mind was closed off. *Telepathically immune? I've heard of that, but they're rare. Never thought I'd meet one.*

Brandon felt a protective surge of emotion that surprised him. Whatever made the stranger fearful brought up a primal defensiveness that Brandon had never felt before. In moose form, he would have lowered his head, shaken his antlers, and bellowed.

With no visible threat, there wasn't much Brandon could do. No one in the aisle seemed to be paying the stranger any attention, and since Brandon knew all the people from town, he didn't think they were the source of the man's uneasiness.

Feel that? It's because he's our mate.

We haven't even met him. And human-shifter bonds aren't common.

They aren't unknown, either. And he's a catch. A guy that handsome—I can handle it if he doesn't grow antlers. For all we know, he might be hung like a moose. Ha.

Behave, Brandon chided his other half. He realized he had stopped moving in the middle of the aisle and tried to look like he was searching for something on the shelves before anyone noticed.

Get a grip. I'm too old to be twitterpated by a good-looking man.

Not when he's our mate, his inner moose singsonged.

Brandon started forward and, accidentally on purpose, bumped into the stranger's shoulder.

"Sorry." His nervous blush was genuine, even if the incident was intentional.

"No problem," the other man replied in a low rumble of a voice that made Brandon's dick twitch. "Do you happen to know where the microwave popcorn is?"

Brandon met the clearest blue eyes he had ever seen and almost forgot how to speak. "I think it's in the next aisle, next to the nuts." He felt as tongue-tied as he had at his first prom.

"Thanks," the stranger said with a smile that made Brandon's heart rate spike.

Brandon tried to keep walking and look nonchalant, only to step on his own bootlace and nearly trip.

Smooth. Real smooth. Now if he remembers me, he'll remember I'm a dork.

Where are we going? That's our mate! Can't you tell by the scent? his moose shouted.

What do you want me to do—throw him over my shoulder and carry him off?

If necessary. Don't let him wander away!

Brandon agreed with his other half's interest but couldn't figure out a way to keep the man in his sights, short of kidnapping.

He admitted to lingering longer than he needed to so he could watch for when the handsome stranger went to a checkout line. The other man's cart held a few dozen staples—peanut butter, bread, ramen, beer, sodas, instant hot chocolate, coffee, some sundries, and several packages of microwave pizza.

Brandon got in line behind the stranger, who had a couple of people ahead of him, so they had to wait.

"New in town or just passing through?" Brandon hoped he sounded off-handed. The other man looked surprised to be spoken to and blushed adorably.

"Does it show that much?"

Brandon smiled. "No, not really. Just an educated guess from your cart. Looks like basic provisioning."

"Busted. Got here last night. Not sure how long I'm staying. Seems like a nice town."

"It's a great place." Brandon tried not to feel overwhelmed by the man's intoxicating scent that already had him half hard. As far as he could tell, the stranger wasn't having any of the same difficulty.

Maybe he's not a shifter. He could be a psychic.

He's our mate. Do something! his inner moose prompted.

"Do you live here? How bad is the winter?"

Brandon chuckled. "Yes, I live here. As for how bad it gets—we've got storms coming in. Smart to load up on essentials, including firewood and batteries, and get a solar cell phone charger if you don't have one already. People actually do get snowed in here."

"Good to know." The man hesitated and put out his hand. "I'm Riley."

Brandon shook and felt a *zing* of connection. From the surprise on Riley's face, he thought something must have registered to him too. "Brandon."

"Nice to meet you." Riley's turn came up at the cashier, taking his attention for several minutes.

Do something. He's getting away, his moose nudged.

"Hey—I don't know how much you like the outdoors, but I'm a

guide." Brandon fished a business card out of his inner jacket pocket. "At the least, I'm happy to answer questions to help you settle in."

"Thanks." Riley pocketed the card. Brandon tried to read the man's expression, but it seemed as closed to him as the other's thoughts. "I just might take you up on that." Their gazes locked, and Brandon thought he saw a hint of mischief, a flicker of interest, and wary caution.

"Hope you do." Brandon hoped he sounded sincere without coming on too strong. His people skills for business were just fine, but he was woefully out of practice when it came to flirting.

Riley turned back to the cashier as Brenda finished ringing him up. "See you around," he said with a grin and a tip of his head.

"See ya." Brandon couldn't help watching as Riley walked away.

"Notice something you like?" Brenda teased. She was around the same age as Brandon's mother.

He cleared his throat. "Just…being friendly."

"Sure you are." Brenda started to ring up Brandon's purchases, and Brandon wondered if Riley had noticed—or questioned—the bale of hay on the bottom of his cart. It wasn't Brandon's first choice for dinner in his other form, but it would do if the storm got too bad for him to venture out.

Brandon wasn't vain, but he knew he cut a handsome figure in his moose. He stood six-foot-five inches at the shoulder, and his antlers spread six feet across and nearly three feet high. Brandon was a trim two-hundred twenty pounds as a human but closer to thirteen hundred as a moose.

"If you want to be 'friendly' some more, check out the poster on the bulletin board at the front doors." She bagged the items as Brandon swiped his credit card. "He's playing in the lounge over at the hotel."

"Really?" Brandon grinned, happy to have a way to follow up on his insta-crush.

"That's what it says on the sheet," Brenda replied. "Guess you'll have to show up and see for yourself."

"Thanks," he said in a sudden hurry. He pushed the cart toward the parking lot and paused in the space between the inside and outside doors to look at the community bulletin board. Posters about upcoming library events vied for space with announcements for craft circles, book clubs, movie nights, and other events. Fox Hollow residents were experts at creating ways to while away the long dark.

There he is. A photocopied poster tacked to the board showed a professional headshot of Riley with his guitar, grinning into the camera. *Riley Henderson, musician in residence at the Fox Hollow Hotel.* Brandon memorized the days and times that Riley played.

Well, that explains why he's here—sort of. This isn't our big tourist season, so he's not going to make bank on tips. Maybe he wanted to get away from the rat race to write songs?

At least I can see him again without being a stalker.

He's our mate. Of course you want to see him again, his moose argued.

Yes, I think he's hot. I'm attracted. But I can't just walk up to him and announce that we're mates.

His moose snorted. *Humans make things complicated.*

How do we even know he'll believe shifters are real? Maybe not everyone thinks "mated to the moose" sounds sexy. They don't write moose shifter romances. Wolves, yeah. Moose? Not so much.

Show off our rack, the moose advised. *We are well-hung.*

Um…that doesn't mean what you think it means. Brandon resisted the urge to face-palm, even if his other side wasn't wrong.

Brandon glanced at the time. Poker night meant he wouldn't have been able to check out Riley's set tonight if he'd already started, but tomorrow night's debut was a definite.

He drove home and put groceries away. The storm wasn't due for a few more days, but Brandon had learned not to take chances with low supplies. While he could forage in his other form if needed, even a full-grown moose could get in trouble in foul weather.

Does Riley know what it's like here in a storm? I wonder where he's living. Somewhere warm, I hope. It can get brutal if you're not prepared. I couldn't read anything from him—not even whether he's a shifter. The weather is worse for humans.

Brandon folded up the reusable grocery bags and made a pot of coffee. He couldn't get Riley out of his mind.

His last relationship with a human park ranger hadn't ended well. They had gotten along famously until Carl found out about Brandon's telepathy. He had been angry and edgy as if he had caught Brandon going through his things. Brandon had tried to explain about shielding and control, that he wouldn't violate boundaries, but Carl's constant suspicion radiated far more than his thoughts.

Brandon hadn't even tried to explain the shifter part.

Brandon, much like his moose, was fairly solitary. He appreciated his poker friends and the other people he had gotten to know in Fox Hollow, but he was just as happy spending an evening reading as he was at a party. Fox Hollow had provided a sanctuary for him to build a life where he could be himself, but it didn't offer a lot of dating choices.

A couple of his guide clients had been tempting, but nothing ever led anywhere. Brandon didn't like hook-ups, in part because tuning out his telepathy was especially difficult during sex, and there was a lot he didn't want to find out about a partner when they were already in bed.

What if I didn't have to worry about the telepathy part? I wouldn't have to spend so much effort locking down my gift, and we could just be together.

There hasn't been much of an upside to being a telepath. People are wary around me and get paranoid about what they're thinking. They pull back. Or I get bombarded with noise if I'm not careful, and I find out things I don't want to know.

Would that be too quiet? I'm used to the background noise of other people's thoughts, even if I'm not trying to listen. I think I could get used to the silence. It might be calming.

All day, Brandon's thoughts strayed back to Riley while he did laundry and went through the mail. *Is he a good kisser? Would he be responsive in bed? What would it feel like to pull him into a hug?* Despite being shorter, Riley still looked solid, although the parka kept Brandon from getting a glimpse of muscles. *I think we could be a good match. But I don't even know if he bats for my team.*

Brandon thought Riley might have flirted back a little, but not enough for Brandon to feel confident making the first move. Being gay wasn't an issue for Fox Hollow regulars, but Riley was new, and Brandon had learned to be cautious.

Maybe I'll get lucky, and I can…get lucky.

2
——————

RILEY

Earlier that day.

RILEY PULLED his Honda Pilot into the space in front of the efficiency apartment rental at the Fox Hollow Lake Motel. The motor lodge looked like it had been around since the 1960s but was well-maintained and refreshed. In summer, Riley guessed that the motel's stretch of beach was probably as popular as the view.

From here, he could look across the ice and glimpse the Victorian hotel where he would be playing, on the other side of a public beach and the seaplane dock.

What the hell was I thinking, coming here in the dead of winter?

It wasn't the first time Riley had questioned his sanity, and might not be the last.

Yeah, yeah. Crazy ex, fresh start, leave the past behind, yada yada.

Tate, Riley's ex, was bad news. They broke up months ago, but Tate kept "coincidentally" popping up too often to be random. Riley had stayed with Tate far too long before making a break, and Tate hadn't taken it well. Privately, Riley suspected that Tate wasn't just an asshole

—he fit the profile for a psi-vamp, someone who could feed on the energy of the people around them.

Recovering was a process, a journey Riley knew he was still making, but he'd made a lot of progress. He hoped that the work he had signed up for with the Fox Institute would help him heal in the ways time alone hadn't.

A friend from Ithaca referred him to the Institute's director, Dr. Rich Jeffries, and put in a good word. Jeffries had been intrigued with Riley's lack of psychic ability. "Nil," he had called it, or "psychic immune." It wasn't just that Riley didn't have psychic abilities of his own; he was also naturally difficult for other psychics to read or influence. Being a 'nil' didn't sound sexy. But it did explain why Riley's friends with paranormal gifts always said that being around him was "calming."

Jeffries got funding for a research study, since nils were rare, and offered a three-month package including a rental efficiency and a stipend, plus a job being the resident musician at the hotel, with the chance to earn extra from side gigs. Riley jumped at the chance to get away from Jamestown and put as much distance between himself and Tate as he could and still stay in New York.

Snowstorms and bad roads should make it harder for Tate to look for me if he has any idea where I've gone. I hope I never see him again.

He had promised himself he would go boy-sober, at least for a while. Getting over Tate took time. Tate didn't go gracefully, and Riley swore he'd spotted his ex in places he had no reason being, stalking him.

It hurt to think he had been "food" to Tate, not a partner. Looking back, Riley suspected Tate had seduced him to have a ready source of energy, not for love. That bothered him even more than the breakup. Riley still hoped to find the right guy but knew he'd be gun-shy for a while.

Riley had read all the "find your true love" horoscopes. As a creative and spontaneous Gemini, he knew that his "ideal" zodiac match was a headstrong and passionate Aries. According to the stargazers, he and his Aries would hit it off with lots of quality time and playfulness, having soulful conversations with plenty of casual physical affection and great communication.

Maybe someday. So far, his prior relationships hadn't delivered on those measures, regardless of his ex's sign. *Maybe Mercury was in retrograde or something.*

He sighed and started to unpack. All his clothes, his guitar, amplifier, recording equipment, and keyboard fit in the back of his Pilot. Anything that didn't fit, he had sold or given away since he wasn't planning to return to Jamestown.

It isn't much, he thought, looking over the suitcases and boxes. *But it's mine.*

Steve from the front office met him at the door to the unit. "I think you'll like this one," he told Riley. "You've got a nice view of the lake, for what it's worth once it snows. Parking right in front. You're not likely to need the AC anytime soon, but the heat works great. On good weather days, you can get delivery from a couple of places in town or drive to the ones who don't. If it's really horrible outside, you've got a fridge and microwave. Slow cookers, coffee pots, popcorn makers, and an air fryer are allowed; just try not to set anything on fire."

"I promise to do my best to avoid that," he told Steve. The other man was about Riley's age, with tawny hair and light brown eyes.

"If you need anything, there's someone at the desk in the office until ten at night. After that, we answer the phone for emergencies, but otherwise, we open at nine in the morning," Steve told him.

"This looks perfect," Riley said. The interior of the room echoed the mid-century modern exterior, with teal curtains and bedspread, a star-shaped wall clock, Danish-style furniture, and other period accents. The "kitschy-comfort" vibe felt comfortable and soothing.

"I know you said you were studying with the Institute and playing at the hotel, but try to have a look around. Fox Hollow has a lot going on in the winter," Steve said. "Those of us who live here year-round are good at making our own fun. If you start at the library, they usually have a good idea of what's happening. The Institute offers a lot of stuff for fun too. It's a friendly place. Don't be a stranger."

Riley knew it would take a while for him to get comfortable and stop looking over his shoulder, but he appreciated Steve's nudge.

"Thanks," he said, surprised at the extra time Steve took to help him feel welcome.

"No problem. Just tell Liam at the library what you're interested in, and if it exists in Fox Hollow, he'll get you connected," Steve told him.

Riley decided to leave the unpacking for later and drive around his new town before it got dark. Fox Hollow had one main road that curved past the lake. He drove to the left and took in the big hotel, seaplane dock, beach, and movie theater, spotting a couple of restaurants as well.

A turn to the right revealed a few more shops, the grocery store, library, police department, a diner, and a frozen custard stand with a sign promising to return in the spring.

Then he spotted the comics store and knew he was going to like it here.

A bell over the door jangled when Riley walked inside. The converted house held racks of comic books, shelves packed with everything from lunchboxes to Funko Pops, a big section on the back wall with a sign proclaiming "Manga," and another wall of anime DVDs.

I know one place I'll be spending my money.

"Hi! Welcome to The Book Bunker. Can I help you find anything?" A slender, red-haired man popped out from behind one of the racks holding a stack of comics Riley guessed he had been shelving.

"Oh, give me fifteen minutes, and I'm sure I'll want to buy everything," Riley confessed. "Great store you've got here."

"Thanks. My partner and I run it. I'm Madden." The quick-moving redhead made Brandon think of a squirrel, and he wondered if Madden was a shifter. Riley had a friend back in Jamestown who believed shifters were real. And Dr. Jeffries had said that Fox Hollow was a safe haven for psychics *and* shifters. If Tate could be a psi-vamp, why couldn't shifters exist? It was just a lot to take in. Though if Riley had met any, they hadn't let their secret slip.

"I'm Riley. I'm new in town. Just getting my bearings."

"Oh! You're going to love it here. Let me show you around the store, and then I'm happy to answer any questions you have about the merchandise or the town," Madden said.

"That would be great. Thank you. I literally just got here today," Riley admitted.

"Good thing. There are storms coming. I bet everyone's told you that, right?"

Riley chuckled. "Just about. People seem worried."

Madden's face switched among several expressions in a second. "Maybe not worried as much as very cautious," Madden said. "When we get a big snowfall, we can be cut off from the outside for days. Cell phones generally stay up, but some folks keep landlines just in case. People have generators because electricity can go out. The biggest thing is having food and plenty of blankets to stay warm."

"Thanks for the tip. The weather here is definitely different from the southern part of the state," Riley replied.

"Have you been around the town yet?" Madden looked eager to share. "You've got to stop at the Bear Necessities coffee shop. My friend Jack is the baker there—his donuts are to die for. For a small town, we've got great food. Can't go wrong with the Full Moon Diner. We've got a brewery and a frozen custard stand, and the bar at the Fox Hollow Hotel has great wings."

"Sounds like you're happy here." Riley hoped Fox Hollow would work its magic on him.

"Love it! Elias and I moved here from Pittsburgh. The weather is colder, but the people are fantastic," Madden swore. Riley suspected that the red-haired man only functioned at full intensity, which was charming.

I'll have to ask Dr. Jeffries how to tell who is and who isn't a shifter. Do they have a secret handshake?

If Madden picked up on Riley's lack of psychic connection, it didn't show. Given the town's history, Riley wondered if he would become a curiosity as those with abilities wondered why he was psychically "mute."

"Your store has an awesome selection," Riley remarked, looking around. "And a big manga section."

"People in Fox Hollow love to read," Madden said. "That's why our library is such a hub of activity. We have decent Wi-Fi—it's been a community priority—so downloading e-books isn't usually a problem unless the power or the towers are out. But lucky for us, folks here also love paper books. You can still read them with a candle in a bad storm, which I guess you wouldn't need for an e-reader." Madden shrugged.

"I haven't had a chance to read manga for a while. Can you suggest some series to get me started again?" Riley didn't want to admit that he stopped reading manga because Tate teased him mercilessly, not because he lost interest. Over the last few months, Riley had done his best to reconnect with the things he loved but set aside because of Tate, and it felt like reclaiming himself.

"Come this way," Madden said dramatically, walking backward and making "follow me" gestures. "I'll lead you right to the Dark Side."

Madden knew his stuff. Riley was impressed as Madden suggested series after series, able to give a good synopsis and make comparisons.

"How's the TV reception up here?" Riley asked.

"Most people have satellite," Madden replied. "Streaming works—except when it doesn't. I wouldn't count on sitting out the big storm watching TV."

"What's your favorite show?" Riley was pleased to have found someone who shared his interests.

"Other than the anime I mentioned, we watch a lot of mysteries and Korean dramas. But my go-to show is *Paranormal*. You know—the one where the two guys travel all over hunting monsters? That's actually how Elias and I met. I write fan fiction about the show, and Elias read my stories, and we ended up connecting in real life. Crazy, huh?"

Riley shrugged. "I've heard crazier. It's nice to have things in common with a partner."

He couldn't help thinking about how he and Tate shared very few interests, and Tate often made fun of him where their fandoms diverged. Taking back those interests felt defiant.

"If you ever want to hang out, we have RPG—Role Playing Game —nights on Tuesdays. The games change each week. Mostly tabletop. Some of our regulars also run video game campaigns and open up for new members. We'd love to have you come try it out," Madden offered.

"Thank you. I might do that once I get settled in." Riley appreciated Madden's effort to bring him into the community.

"Mico and Jack are regulars. Jack's the one who makes the donuts," Riley said. "With Elias and me, that's generally four, and we sometimes get a few more. It varies week to week."

Riley had to admit that the game night sounded fun. When he wasn't studying or involved in the research program—or playing at the hotel—it could be a good way to meet people and make friends.

His scholarship currently covered three months, with the option to renew. Riley couldn't help hoping that he could parlay the opportunity into something permanent. Despite the weather warnings, he liked what he had seen of Fox Hollow and had never met a friendlier group of people.

Riley brought his purchases to the counter, and Madden rang him up. "Here's a schedule for game nights and the other events we have scheduled." Madden slipped a sheet into the bag. "Come back soon! Don't be a stranger!"

Riley promised to return and headed back to his car. He had initially been worried that playing music at a hotel restaurant in the dead of winter would mean thin crowds and poor tips. But everything seemed to suggest Fox Hollow residents worked hard at staying connected and being social.

Happy with his purchases, Riley drove back to the hotel and tried to squash the nervousness in his belly over his new gig.

The Fox Hollow Hotel faced the lake, a four-story Victorian that looked more polished than the log cabin style Riley had expected. He vaguely remembered reading that wealthy people from smoky cities came for the fresh air back in the 1900s and left behind upscale cottages and lodges.

Riley parked the Pilot and took a deep breath before he cut off the ignition and got out. The brisk wind off the lake jolted him awake after the warmth of the SUV.

He jogged up the steps, noting the wide porch and rocking chairs that would be prime spots for lake watching in good weather, and hurried into the lobby. An old-fashioned wooden check-in desk sat to one side, with groupings of couches and armchairs on the other, clustered around a large fireplace with a roaring blaze. *Cozy rustic chic*, he thought, appreciating the welcoming atmosphere.

"Hi, I'm Riley Henderson—the new musician," he told the man behind the counter. "I'm supposed to see Dennis Todd. He's expecting me."

"Welcome to Fox Hollow," the desk clerk replied. "Please have a seat in the lobby. I'll let Mr. Todd know that you're here."

Riley walked around the lobby looking at the landscape paintings of idyllic forest scenes and tall mountains. The Victorian furnishings looked comfortable but durable—not as fancy as a city hotel.

He stopped in front of the stone fireplace. Its heat forced him to stand six feet away and warmed him quickly.

"Riley?"

Riley turned to see an older man striding toward him. He wore a sweater over a collared shirt and khaki pants with Keen boots.

"Mr. Todd?" Riley stepped forward and shook his new boss's hand.

"Did you have any trouble getting here?" Todd asked. "You have good timing—there are storms coming our way, as you've no doubt heard."

Riley chuckled. "It's been mentioned once or twice."

"Did you get settled in? Dr. Jeffries said he had you set up over at the motel. We thought that might allow you some distance and privacy rather than staying here, and they have efficiency apartments," Todd said with the enthusiasm Riley was coming to consider a hallmark of Fox Hollow residents.

"I dropped off my stuff at the motel, and I'm heading to the grocery store after this," Riley assured him. "It won't take me long to settle in."

"Good to hear. Let me give you a tour, and you can ask me whatever you want to know. Have you seen Jeffries yet?"

Riley shook his head. "No. I have an appointment with him in the morning to go over my classes and the scholarship."

Todd nodded. "He'll have the paperwork for the work-study position here as a musician. We're very excited to have you entertaining with us. The crowds at this time of year aren't the largest, but people value the chance to get out of the house and congregate—assuming the roads have been plowed. You'll also be working with

Tyler Williams. He's the assistant manager. His family owns the hotel."

As Todd showed him around the hotel, Riley felt himself falling a little bit in love with the historic building. The public rooms all had a comfortable Victorian décor, period-authentic without the excesses of the time. High-backed velvet couches and chairs in the lobby, an intricate mantle over the fireplace, and lots of pine wainscoting gave an upscale feeling while still fitting the "rustic chic" vibe.

"We have three restaurants here in the hotel," Todd told him. "Our main dining room and our bar are where you'll play most of the time. There's a patio eating area and outdoor bar, but they're closed most of the winter unless we're having a special event, like the snowmobile race."

The main restaurant was a white tablecloth kind of place, with a nice view of the lake through huge windows. That contrasted with the main bar, which had a massive barback and carved wood counter that sported a brass footrail. Sconces and another fireplace made the area feel cozy and hunt-club-style luxurious.

"We aren't packed in the off-season, but we do have a mix of guests and locals that keep us busy," Todd told him. "Especially when the snow makes people want to stay close to home."

As they walked around the hotel, Riley felt his enthusiasm grow. He enjoyed playing in more intimate settings where his acoustic guitar and keyboards could shine. While people would be going on with their meals and conversations as he played, Riley knew live music added an important element to the experience.

"And of course, if you're approached by people to play for private events, that's perfectly okay. We just ask that you not accept gigs with other hotels in a twenty-mile radius. We want to keep you to ourselves," Todd added with a smile.

"That's completely understandable." Riley thought the terms were very reasonable, especially since the job had been arranged by the Institute to augment his stipend.

"That's the tour," Todd said as they returned to the lobby. "Have you gotten the lay of the land yet for town? Fox Hollow does a good job of having the basics people need close at hand. That's especially nice during the winter when no one wants to drive to a big box store for necessities. Plenty to do, too, for the nights you're not playing or studying."

"I'm really excited to be here." Riley hoped he wasn't gushing. "It'll be fun getting to know people." *And maybe I'll meet someone. It could happen.*

"Come in an hour before your set to get everything in place," Todd said. "You're the only musician, so we can leave your amps and big gear set up. That way you don't have to break it down each time and haul it back and forth. We'll make sure it's safe."

That took a worry off Riley's mind since he had pictured himself manhandling speakers in knee-deep snow.

"I'll see you tomorrow." Riley shook Todd's hand.

He left with a spring in his step, excited about what he had seen. That meant just one more stop before he went back to the motel and settled in. Riley planned to stay in tonight, leaving exploring for another day when he wasn't tired from the drive. He figured he would find something on television, and if not, he had plenty of books on his e-reader and some paperbacks in his duffle. The new books he got at the comics store were going to the top of his pile.

Fox Hollow Grocery didn't look fancy from the outside, but as soon as he stepped inside, Riley felt amazed by the sheer variety of items the store stocked. He grabbed a cart and began working his way around the aisles slowly, looking for the items on his list and making mental notes of what he might need to buy in the near future.

The smell of baking bread tempted him from the bakery, and the produce aisle was remarkably fresh, considering the season. Riley wasn't planning on cooking any fancy dinners with his minimal kitchen, but the meat counter offered mouth-watering options. He picked up basics—peanut butter, jelly, bread, lunch meat and sandwich fixings, chips, coffee, and a few other staples just in case he really did get snowed in.

A couple of frozen entrees and small pizzas got added to the cart, next to a case of beer. He had brought a few fifths of whiskey with him and figured he would have time to figure out where the nearest liquor store was before his stash ran low.

Where do they keep the microwave popcorn?

Someone bumped into him, and Riley looked up—and up. The dark-haired man was at least three or four inches taller, with broad shoulders. Dark brown eyes widened as their gazes met.

Riley registered a couple of things in those first few seconds. The stranger was handsome, probably hid an amazing body beneath his parka, and had the prettiest eyes Riley had ever seen.

"Sorry." The stranger sounded adorably embarrassed.

"No problem," Riley stammered. "Do you know where the microwave popcorn is?" he blurted.

Tall Guy told him, and Riley thanked him, not sure how to carry on the conversation he wanted to have while standing in a grocery aisle.

Smooth move, he berated himself. *That was the hottest guy I've seen in a long time, and all I could do was ask about popcorn?*

Then again, it's a small town. I'm likely to see him again.

Aargh. And he'll remember me as "popcorn man."

Riley felt a surge of excitement as Tall Guy lined up behind him in the checkout lane. They chatted about the town and the weather. Riley admitted that he was new but didn't mention the gig at the hotel.

"I'm a wilderness guide." The man passed Riley a card. "I'd be happy to show you around or just answer questions."

"Thank you." Riley pocketed the card. The clerk asked for his credit card, Riley paid and the moment passed.

"See you around," Riley said as he finished at the counter. There didn't seem to be a way to continue without being awkward, so he walked away, wishing he was smoother with the pickup lines.

Then again, he gave me his card.

Once Riley got in the car, he looked at the card. *Brandon Davis, Wilderness Guide. Hikes, overnights, fishing, canoe trips. Call for rates,* followed by Brandon's phone number and email.

I'm not really an outdoor jock. Would a guy like him be interested in a guy like me? Then again, they say opposites attract.

Riley thought about Brandon as he returned to the motel and unpacked his groceries. He liked men who were taller and solidly built. The dark eyes and floppy hair were sexy in a slightly dorky way.

Just because he gave me his card doesn't mean he's gay or interested. He might just see a new potential client.

Still, Brandon ended up behind Riley in line and started up the conversation again, making sure to pass along his contact information. Riley decided to take it as a good sign and see if he ran into Brandon again soon.

Riley tried out the diner and enjoyed their excellent meatloaf. He couldn't help but look around for Brandon but didn't see him. Riley felt restless when he went back to the motel and flipped through the channels on the television, but nothing caught his attention, and he was too jittery to read.

He sprawled on his bed and slipped a hand down his pants, wrapping his fingers around his cock. Riley was already half-hard just from thinking about Brandon, even though he only had those few moments at the grocery store.

Deep voice. Tall. Big hands. Bet he's proportional. I wonder if I could see his moose knuckle in tight pants. Hmm. I like the sound of that.

Those shoulders…yummy. It would be nice being with someone larger for a change. I can deal with being the little spoon.

Riley's hand moved more quickly, slicked by the pre-come he leaked picturing the body that might have been concealed by all those layers.

He's a wilderness guy, so I bet he's got a fantastic body. Nice pecs, solid arms, great thighs.

Riley couldn't explain the *zing* he felt when their hands met, but he figured it was probably static electricity—although he wanted to think it was a touch of fate.

Wonder if he tops or bottoms—or switches? Hope he's vers. I'd love to have him every which way.

After a long day and the tension of arriving in a new place, Riley's orgasm crested much more quickly than he wanted, carrying him over the top and fountaining over his fist.

Happily sated, Riley wiped himself off with his T-shirt and collapsed onto the bed.

So much for boy-sober. Still, there's no guarantee he's actually interested.

Or that he really bats for my team. Or that we'd have anything in common aside from attraction. But I'd sure like to find out.

3

BRANDON

By the time he drove over to Russ's house for the poker game, Brandon had made up his mind to see whether the attraction to Riley was mutual. And if he could learn more about Riley from his friends, all the better.

"The beer is here, and the moose is loose," Brandon proclaimed when he walked into the kitchen, adding his bag to a pile of contributions that included chips, dip, cookies, and other favorite snacks.

"Pizza's in the oven, and the fox has socks!" Liam greeted him, raising one foot to show off his very bright striped socks.

"Nothing rhymes with 'wolf' so get over it." Russ joined them in the kitchen and gave Liam a peck on the lips. "Good to see you, Brandon. Come on in."

The cabin had originally belonged to a friend of his grandfather's, who sold it to Russ when the wolf brothers had a big argument with their father over being gay. Since then, Russ had expanded the cabin with a bigger bathroom and a shower big enough for two.

All of which came in handy when he and Liam moved in together and Drew hit it off with Noah. Brandon had heard them talk about building a second cabin, but that wasn't going to happen before spring.

They talked and joked waiting for the pizza to bake and polished off dinner before settling in for their game.

The poker table was set up in the living room, and everyone took their seats. Russ dealt. Their game night had gone on for years, low stakes so no one had to worry about losing rent money.

"Looks like I'm grounded for a while with those storms," Justin, the blond sea plane pilot, noted. "Just as well. If I'm snowed in, I'll have to work on the repair projects I've been putting off."

"The library will open as usual, but we'll be watching the situation, and we'll close if the snow comes in like they say it's going to." Liam placed chips to make his bet.

"The garage is doing the same thing," Drew added. "Personally, I think we're going to get a snowpocalpyse, but it wouldn't be the first time a storm blew right past us." Seeing the Lowe brothers together made the family resemblance clear, Brandon thought.

"I have one more booking and then nothing until the following week, so we'll see if the storms blow over," Brandon said. "Got a group that wants to cross-country ski some of the trails and do an overnight."

He paused, hoping to sound off-handed. "Anyone hear about the new musician at the Fox Hollow Hotel?"

Tyler nodded. "He's doing a work-study program with the Fox Institute, and the gig at the hotel is part of that. Riley Henderson. Seems like a nice guy—and he's a good musician. I heard his audition videos. I think having him will give people an incentive to come hang out at the restaurant and bar."

Riley Henderson. Brandon filed the name away to look up his videos.

"I saw the posters tacked up at the grocery store," Brandon said. "And I ran into Riley in the check-out line."

Liam looked up, giving Brandon a sly glance. "Did our moose see something he likes?"

"We just chatted in line," Brandon deflected, but he felt his ears warm with a blush.

"Uh-huh." Liam turned back to his cards. "You'll never know if you don't try."

"He might be some kind of psychic, but that doesn't mean he knows about shifters," Brandon offered in weak protest.

"If he sticks around for long, he'll figure it out," Drew noted. "Jeffries wouldn't have offered him a scholarship if he didn't think Riley would fit in here."

That made Brandon happy to think that Riley might like Fox Hollow enough to stay.

"He's staying over at the motel," Tyler volunteered. "That gives him an efficiency apartment and a little space from the crowd where he plays. We should make sure he has a good audience."

"I hope he can take the cold," Noah said. "He doesn't seem like the 'camping in the rough' sort of guy."

Despite the good-natured ribbing, Brandon knew his friends would be supportive if he and Riley got together. *Now I just have to get over my nerves and ask him out.*

They talked as they played. Brandon kept them laughing with funny things that happened on his last couple of tours, and told them about the multi-day cross-country skiing trip he had coming up.

"Our next big thing is the Winter Moose Festival," Liam said. "It's taken a lot of planning, but things are finally coming together."

Fox Hollow celebrated the designated days for a lot of animals—wolves, squirrels, bear, possums, raccoons, and more, trying to include all the shifters in town.

"We'll have a read-a-thon of moose-themed books, like that one about the muffin," Liam went on, excited to share the plans. "Then there's a sing-a-long of songs about moose as well as a picture exhibition from the art classes at the library. And of course, the *Rocky and Bullwinkle* cartoon marathon at the theater."

"Want to see me pull a rabbit out of my hat?" Brandon joked in his best impersonation of Bullwinkle.

Liam rolled his eyes. "That would be impressive, I'm sure. There's also a 'Moose and Myth' seminar at the Fox Institute, and the Loyal Order of Moose are doing a charity fundraiser."

"I still think that you should need to *be* a moose to join that group," Brandon grumbled good-naturedly.

"And don't forget the Moose Trails walk that Brandon is leading," Liam added.

"I think it sounds like a great event," Russ said. "Although I'm a little scared to find out what you've got planned for Wolf Week."

Liam gave Russ a devilish grin. "Just wait. It's going to be amazing."

Russ groaned. "That's what I'm afraid of."

"I'm going to ask Riley if he'll play for the sing-a-long," Liam said. "I should have enough money in the budget to pay him."

"Are there that many moose songs?" Noah asked.

Drew elbowed him. "Probably more moose songs than lynx ones. Moose rhymes better."

Of course. Because moose are noble creatures of the forest worthy of adoration, Brandon's inner moose said in a smug tone.

They ate pizza, drank beer, and munched on chips, with plenty of good-natured razzing between hands of cards. By the end of the game, Brandon had broken even, and Noah was the night's winner of forty dollars.

"Just enough to take my sweetie out for dinner at the diner." Noah gathered his winnings.

"So romantic," Drew replied, but he looked pleased.

"See you next week?" Russ asked as he and Liam started to gather empty bottles and plates.

"Sure thing," Brandon said, and the others echoed his answer.

The short drive home in the cold woke Brandon after the warmth of Russ's cabin and a couple of beers. No longer sleepy, Brandon grabbed his laptop and went looking for Riley's music online.

He found Riley's website and a video playlist. Riley did a mix of music, covering mellow favorites and tossing in what Brandon suspected were original songs. While some of the tunes would get an audience clapping along and echoing the chorus, others were wistful ballads.

Our mate has a beautiful voice, his moose spoke up after having been mostly silent all evening.

He sure does. Hearing Riley's voice and watching the emotions on his face as he performed stirred a mix of lust, possessiveness, and longing that Brandon had never felt before.

Brandon had casually dated, but nothing seemed to stick. He didn't like hook-ups, and the closest gay bar was in Lake George, not exactly convenient. After his last relationship broke up, Brandon started to wonder whether there was someone out there for him, especially after several of his friends found their fated mates.

I've just been alone too long. I've forgotten what it feels like to have a crush.

Sure. Tell that to yourself, but I'm not buying it, his moose challenged. *He's ours—and you know it.*

Doesn't matter if I know it. I have to get Riley to fall in love with me—and so far, I've sucked at getting crushes to return my interest.

Try sucking something else, his shifter suggested in a sly tone.

Ha, ha. Not funny.

As a moose, Brandon felt handsome and confident. He knew he cut an imposing form, huge and tall, with an impressive spread of antlers.

As plain old human Brandon, he felt awkward and gangly, likely to get his feet tangled up or trip on his shoelace. His chestnut hair always seemed to fall in his eyes, and when he wasn't guiding a group or with friends, he often felt at a loss for words.

Look how good Riley is with the crowd, he thought, paying close attention to how Riley interacted with his audience in the video. *I could never do something like that.*

We don't need two musicians in the family, his moose argued. *Betcha being a guide makes more than being a musician. So, we bring in the big bucks, and he makes sure we have someone warm to come home to.*

That sounds like a 1950s sitcom, Brandon argued. *A big part of this is going to depend on if Riley wants to stay in Fox Hollow and what he wants to do when his time with the Institute is over.*

Brandon couldn't help feeling curious about what led Riley to seek out training with the Fox Institute, and how that worked with his telepathic barriers. *Is he a psychic immune? And if so, would that be restfully quiet or would I get lonely not being able to hear my mate in my mind?*

You'll never know until you try, his moose said, encouraging and a little wistful.

Before I start anything—assuming he's even interested—

He is. Are you blind when you're human? That scent—he's our mate.

Assuming that's true, what if he is only human? Maybe a psychic immune, but not a shifter. Is that enough for you? Not another moose or even an animal we can run with in the woods. Just human. And a human who might be blocked to our telepathy. We might have a mating bond, but it won't be like with another moose and without the intimacy of being able to know his thoughts?

Could you live with that? Because it's not fair to either him or me to start what we aren't going to finish.

It would be good not to be alone. Even if our mate is "just" human. Even if he's silent. It would be enough for me. Is it enough for you?

I don't know—but I want to find out.

It had occurred to Brandon that acceptance wasn't a one-way street. Riley might be accepting of psychic talents, but having a partner who turned into an antlered creature the size of a car? Sure, letting Riley witness a shift would get past the "seeing is believing" part, but what then?

Madden said his partner is a regular human, and they seem to be doing okay.

We couldn't frolic in our fur together, but would it matter?

Brandon wanted to believe he and Riley could get past that if everything else was good. Fox Hollow had plenty of "mixed" marriages—carnivore and herbivore, small animal and large, different species, psychic and shifter. He found himself hoping that he and Riley might be able to find something uniquely them.

I need a game plan. It's been a long time since I've asked anyone out on a date.

Atta boy. Too long. We're rusty, his moose cheered.

Not helping. You don't know anything I don't know.

I know moose things. Where to find the best berries and twigs, how to cross a river—

None of which help when it comes to romance. And Riley already works at the nicest restaurant in town. I can't take him there. I need to think about how to do this.

Don't think about it too long. We aren't getting any younger.

On that note, Brandon let his connection to his other half go quiet, already feeling outvoted. He decided to sleep on the problem and come up with a plan in the morning.

He couldn't help daydreaming as he got ready for bed. *If Riley returned his interest, would they take it slow or fall head-over-heels? What if Riley didn't stay in Fox Hollow? Could falling for each other give Riley a reason not to leave when his time with the Institute was over?*

Brandon tried to quiet his thoughts when he slipped into bed, but he lay awake listening to Riley's music videos on repeat, falling a little more in love with that beautiful voice with each song.

He reached for his half-hard cock and got the lube out of the nightstand. Brandon stared at the screen watching the close-ups of Riley's face, his soulful eyes and pouting lips.

I bet he's an amazing kisser. I'd like to feel those lips all over. I bet he gives head as good as he kisses.

Brandon closed his eyes, focusing on Riley's voice and the memory of his face. He slicked his hand and slipped his fist along his cock from root to crown, then jacked himself slowly, wanting the feeling to build, holding himself off from a quick finish.

On some lyrics, Riley's voice soared, while others were a gritty growl that set Brandon's whole body on fire. He picked up the pace, letting his thumb swipe over the head, pressing that sensitive spot just beneath the flare, running his nail lightly through the slit.

Brandon groaned and used his left hand to push his sleep pants down farther so he could lightly tug on his balls as he kept up the rhythm with his right hand.

In his mind, he imagined Riley naked in bed with him, eyes dark with lust, a light sheen of sweat covering his body, lips parted and plump.

"Please," Brandon murmured, and in his fantasy, Riley slithered down the bed and wrapped that beautiful mouth around Brandon's hard, leaking cock, taking his sizeable prick down in one swallow.

"Riley." Brandon stroked himself faster, lasting only a few more times before his climax ripped through him, and he shot all over his hand.

His orgasm was intense enough that Brandon lay still for a couple of minutes in the afterglow, spent and happily relaxed.

Sticky, cooling come motivated him to use his shirt to clean up, tossing it toward the laundry bag in the closet and grabbing his tee from earlier as a replacement.

Riley's soulful voice still streamed from Brandon's phone. He watched, entranced, as Riley put his whole heart into the music.

Why is he so sad? It seems like more than just a performance. Did someone hurt him? Maybe there's more to his decision to come to Fox Hollow than taking classes and a work-study scholarship.

The idea of someone harming Riley sent a spike of possessive heat through Brandon so sharp it took him by surprise.

Mate. No one hurts our mate, his moose growled.

Easy there. Maybe he's just a good actor. If I could even surface-read him, I'd know for sure.

Protect. He needs us.

I'd like to think so, but we don't know yet.

Green leaves quickly wither, and opportunity is quickly lost, his moose responded.

Is that some sort of moose wisdom?

The First Ones say moose are wise, strong, and noble, his other half said with a sniff.

Keep telling yourself that.

Brandon's attention returned to the handsome man singing his heart out on the video. *Tomorrow night, we'll go watch him play. And see how things go.*

His promise soothed his shifter half, and Brandon let Riley's video sing him to sleep.

Brandon had another day before his trail hike, which he used to lay in provisions, replenish the emergency supplies in his backpack, and get everything in order.

Once that was done, he found himself at loose ends. Storm warnings still had everyone on edge, but his clients didn't cancel, and

Brandon hoped they would get lucky and finish before the storm came. If the forecast changed and the snow moved in early, he would have to reschedule, but for now, it looked like they had a window of time to make it work.

After Brandon finished the preparations, he walked to a sheltered grove behind his cabin where he had built a cabana with a wood stove for warmth and towels for wet weather. Smaller shifters could make their change indoors and scoot out the back door, but that didn't work for a moose—which made for a cold transition to his four-legged form.

He lit the stove and undressed, shivering despite the quickly building fire.

Someday, I'm going to remember to start the stove early so I don't have to drop trou in knee-deep snow.

His shift wasn't quick. Brandon had seen smaller creatures make the change—otters, dogs, forest cats, and similarly-sized animals and birds transformed relatively fast—not nearly the grueling process Hollywood werewolf movies portrayed.

Changing into a moose, on the other hand, took a bit more work. Brandon had long ago given up trying to understand the physics behind the shift, chalking it up to magic. No doubt scholars at the Fox Institute had done the equations and calculated how such a thing was possible, but Brandon didn't care.

The frigid air that made him shiver as a man didn't faze his moose. Brandon stood to his full height and gave his massive rack of antlers a shake. His long legs and sharp hooves had no difficulty with the snow in all but the most extreme weather.

Brandon left the shelter and headed into the woods. He stretched his neck to reach the tenderest twigs and new growth. His supple lips and strong tongue expertly stripped every bit of edible growth, which he chewed as he ventured farther into the woods.

It took a lot to feed him in moose form. Unless he had a lazy Saturday to roam the forest and snack to his heart's content, Brandon ate enough to stop his inner moose from nagging and then got his fill as a human, where his appetite was easier and cheaper to accommodate.

Once he had eaten enough, he found a spot with a nice view where he could stand and ruminate, slowly digesting the roughage and chewing the cud. That process provided good thinking time, a chance for Brandon to quiet his human thoughts and let his moose mind focus on the sounds and smells of the forest around him.

The wind stirred branches in the tree next to where he stood, sending down a shower of snow. Brandon chuffed and shook it off, aided by a slick, dense coat that was nearly waterproof.

Nature feels different when I'm a moose.

Different how? his moose asked, not snarky for once.

I see better as a human, but I can smell and hear more as a moose.

We're taller, bigger, faster, stronger. There's a lot to like about being a moose, his shifter side defended.

Absolutely. But there're are a lot of good things about being human too.

Like what? his moose challenged.

Soft bedsheets, a good mattress, a hot shower, Brandon replied. *Coffee. Donuts. And I can't play video games with hooves.*

Okay, I'll give you that.

After a while, Brandon felt ready to go back. He shifted as quickly as he could, which still left his naked human form hopping from foot to foot in front of the blazing stove as he lost his protective moose bulk. Brandon grabbed his clothes and dressed, hurrying into his parka and boots.

He banked the stove so it would burn down and headed inside for a late breakfast of human food. Hot coffee, fluffy pancakes, and warm applesauce got rid of any remaining chill. The smell of maple syrup made Brandon hard remembering the maple and anise scent he had picked up from Riley at the store.

Face facts—we've got it bad for him, his moose said.

Brandon sighed, sounding a lot like his moose snuffle. *I know. I've never felt this much this fast, so it must be a mate bond. You know what I'm usually like with a new boyfriend.*

Clueless?

Enough with your smartass comments.

That's "smart moose," thank you very much.

I meant "cautious." I usually overthink everything and second-guess myself and lose my shot, Brandon replied.

That's where rut makes it easy. Just go with the call of nature.

And be a mindless stud? No thanks.

Fortunately, such things didn't govern the human side of moose shifters, and Brandon had medicine to blunt the impact when he did shift during the season.

After the sexy fantasy Brandon had the previous evening, he couldn't wait to see Riley again. He wasn't sure how to reconnect since Riley would be busy with his performance.

I gave him my card. He hasn't called. Is that a hint that he's not interested?

He's new, just getting settled in, starting a new job. I need to let him catch his breath and not read anything into it. Maybe if he sees me show up at his performances, he'll get a clue that I'm interested.

Since his chores were done and he had the whole afternoon before Riley's show, Brandon decided to drive into town. He stopped at the comics store as if his SUV had a mind of its own.

"Hey, Brandon! Good to see you! We've gotten a bunch of new books in since you were here. Go check them out. If we get the snow they're predicting, you'll have plenty of time to read!" Madden Reid greeted him.

Brandon had rarely seen anyone who resembled their shifter side so much when human as Madden did. The energetic red squirrel always seemed like he had just drunk a whole pot of coffee. Brandon could easily imagine a flicking tail and twitching whiskers from Madden's quick movements.

He looked around and found the shop otherwise empty for the moment. "Can I ask you a question?"

"Sure." Madden grinned. "Whatever I don't know, we can ask Elias or look up. Shoot."

Brandon shifted from foot to foot, feeling self-consciousness kick in. "It's not about comics." He dropped his voice. "It's about falling for a human."

"Ohhh." Madden's eyebrows shot up, and his mouth formed a perfect circle. "Does this mean you met someone? That's so awesome!"

Brandon sighed. "It's not awesome until something actually happens."

Madden motioned for Brandon to follow him to a small seating area where they could talk, and Madden could still watch the door. "Do tell!"

Brandon recounted meeting Riley at the store, the "spark" that passed between them when they touched hands, and the amazing scent he had never smelled before, as well as the way he couldn't stop thinking about Riley.

Madden grinned. "Yep, you've got it bad, Big Guy."

"I know. But I'm pretty sure Riley isn't a shifter. And my telepathy doesn't work on him. I can't even get the most superficial surface read of his thoughts, just some vague emotions. He's…blank. I've never run into that before."

Madden frowned. "So, he's got a scholarship to do a course of study at the Fox Institute, but he's not a psychic and not a shifter? What's left?"

Brandon had mulled over the possibilities, and come up with one answer. "Psychic nils are rare. They are people who have such strong natural shielding that they don't 'broadcast' their thoughts the way most people do unless they've had training."

Madden nodded. "You told me once that for you, it's like everybody is carrying a radio that's tuned into a different channel and playing out loud."

"Pretty much. I've learned to screen out most of it—had to, to not go bonkers," Brandon admitted. "But I always expected to have a mental bond with a mate as well as a physical one. I'm afraid I'll miss it if I can't."

"I don't know about that. Sometimes people need a little space to sort through what's upset them so they don't say things they don't really mean," Madden replied.

"Elias is human. You're a shifter. You told me once he didn't even like squirrels when you first met," Brandon countered, mentioning Madden's partner.

"And then my squirrel saved his life, and he had to reconsider," Madden said with a hint of pride in his voice. "So save Riley's life when you're a moose, and the problem is solved."

Brandon chuckled. "It would be nice if we could get together without mortal danger to either one of us. Is it hard being mated to someone who can't shift? I don't mean to pry—well, not too much—but I don't know who else to ask, and I don't want to talk myself out of something good."

Madden clasped his hands in his lap. "First off, don't worry about prying, but don't blame me if you get TMI. Second—definitely don't talk yourself out of going after Riley just over the human thing. It doesn't have to be a deal-breaker."

"I'm hoping that since he's here because of the Fox Institute, he might be open-minded enough to believe that shifters are real," Brandon admitted. "That would make some of this easier."

"If he's here for the Institute, then he knows Fox Hollow is a haven for psychics and shifters, so he shouldn't doubt our existence. But he may not have any experience with us, and he may not be able to tell who is and who isn't, especially if his gift doesn't clue him in," Madden replied.

"Does it bother you that you and Elias can't do some things together because he can't shift?" Brandon was still trying to get his mind around mating with someone who couldn't go rambling in the woods with him in moose form.

"You mean chase each other in the park and throw acorns? Scurry up and down trees and drop pine cone bombs?" Madden laughed. "I'm sure that would be fun, but those aren't really essentials. I don't see his lack of shifting as a disability, and he doesn't think what I can do is weird."

"Really?"

Madden nodded. "Sometimes we'll go to the park, and I'll run around while he sits on a bench and reads a book. He keeps an eye out for hawks, and I burn off some energy. I can be a bit intense if you haven't noticed."

"Never crossed my mind," Brandon lied with a broad wink.

"I'm jittery, even for a squirrel," Madden confessed. "Elias loves me anyhow. And I bet that if you really are mates, you and Riley can figure things out too."

"We've got two things to get past—the not-shifter part, and the nil part. I always assumed that telepathy would be part of the mate bond," Brandon said. "I've spent my whole life tuning people out, and now the one person who might be my mate isn't broadcasting."

Madden chewed his lip as he thought, and Brandon could almost swear he saw an invisible tail swishing as he concentrated.

"That could be harder," he conceded. "But regular humans go their whole lives without hearing each other's thoughts. We forget that in Fox Hollow, but most people *aren't* psychics and shifters. And they fall in love and get married and grow old together all the time anyhow."

"I never really thought about it like that, but you're right." Brandon felt a spark of hope. He'd gotten discouraged thinking about the obstacles to a relationship with Riley without considering the positives.

"You told me once that it tires you out some days just keeping yourself from hearing all the thoughts around you. Wouldn't it be nice to let down and not worry about that when you're at home with your best boy?"

"I don't have much experience with serious relationships," Brandon confessed. "A couple of those broke up because the people I dated just assumed I listened in on them all the time, and it made them paranoid. I didn't, but that made me wonder what they were hiding. It turned into a clusterfuck."

"Which goes back to what I said—this could be a feature and not a bug," Madden told him. "If you like Riley and think he's your mate, go for it. Dude, you're positively smitten."

Brandon managed a shy smile, feeling his ears burn with embarrassment. "Yeah. I am. Thank you, Madden."

Brandon bought some comics and ran errands before he went home. He remembered the way dream-Riley made him feel and shivered in a way that had nothing to do with the cold.

Could Riley really be my fated mate? I don't want to get my hopes up, but I can't stand the thought of missing my opportunity.

I guess there's only one way to find out. Take a chance...and leap.

4

———

RILEY

The next day, Riley got up early, determined to explore his new temporary home. The desk clerk recommended Bear Necessities Coffee and Café, with a special mention of its donuts. In desperate need of sugar and caffeine, Riley headed there first.

Fox Hollow had one main street shaped like a J that ran alongside the lake before curving inland. The town packed plenty into that space, including shops, a grocery store, library, movie theater, hotel, beach, seaplane landing, outfitter, gift shop, bakery/café, and a couple of restaurants.

Riley wandered into the bear-themed café, smiling at the whimsical artwork of bears having fun doing all sorts of human activities like picnicking, playing music, dancing, and setting off fireworks. The café's few tables had a view of the lake.

He inhaled, enjoying the smell of donuts and fresh coffee in a moment of pure bliss.

"Smell something you want?" A woman in her middle years smiled at him from behind the counter. Her nametag read "Sherri," and her apron read "Bearly In Charge."

"I'm new in town—what do you recommend?"

She looked like she gave his question serious thought for a

moment, then pointed to the donuts in the glass case. "We have an awesome pastry baker who works night shift. These are super-fresh. Everything he makes is good, but his strawberry margherita donuts are my favorites." Sherri pointed to a tray of pink-glazed treats.

"Then again, you can't go wrong with the maple-bacon ones, either. Or get a sampler pack and try them all—you won't regret it," she said with a grin.

"I think I'll take you up on that, and a large latte too, please," Riley said as he peeled off his mittens and pushed his scarf beneath his chin. He had bought a warmer parka for his move north, along with boots better suited to colder temperatures and more snow. He hadn't gotten used to the bulk, and right now he felt like the Michelin Man.

"What brings you to Fox Hollow?" Sherri asked as she got his order ready. With her ample curves and brown hair, Sherri vaguely reminded Riley of a brown bear, like the café's mascot that adorned its sign.

"I'm the new musician for the next few months at the hotel," he told her as he dug out his wallet. "And I'm taking some classes at the Institute."

"Well, you're either going to love it here or hate it because there are some big storms coming our way. We're set up pretty good for such things, so don't let it worry you. Just make sure you've got emergency basics. You'll get used to it if you decide to stay."

Riley paid for his order and looked at the bag. "What do you think I should start with?"

Sherri put her hands on her hips and narrowed her eyes. "Hmm. Everybody has different tastes, but I'm real partial to the maple-bacon even though it isn't the flavor-of-the-day. Jack, our baker, does a great job of coming up with new recipes. It's our sneaky way to make sure you come back to see us often." She winked.

He pulled out one of the maple-bacon donuts and took a bite, then had to stifle an orgasmic moan at the flavors that exploded in his mouth.

"That is the best donut I've ever eaten. I'm a convert."

"Told you so!" Sherri gave a smug grin. "By the way, I'm Sherri, and I own this place with my husband, Nelson. Sheriff Arnel is my cousin."

"I solemnly swear I will always pay for my donuts." Riley crossed his heart with a half-eaten pastry.

"There's a bulletin board just inside the doors where you can tack up a poster if you have something to advertise when you're playing," Sherri said. "Most of Fox Hollow comes through those doors sooner or later."

"Thank you," Riley replied around a mouthful of donut. He had a stack of photocopies for just that purpose and a box of thumbtacks in his coat pocket.

"We have a Coffee Club." Sherri handed him a card with one circle punched. "Every fifth drink gets a free regular coffee, or you can save up seven punches for a specialty coffee."

Riley thanked her and pocketed the card, happily eating his donut as he left. He dodged in and out of the other stores, noting what they carried. The library was next, and Riley carefully closed the donut bag and wiped his hands on his jeans before entering.

The Fox Hollow Library wasn't big, but it looked to Riley as if it utilized every square inch of space. He noted the bulletin board in the foyer and took time to walk around before he went to the front desk.

A slender man with red hair and gold-flecked brown eyes smiled when Riley walked up to the counter. "How can I help you?"

Once again, Riley felt like he got the once-over for being the new kid in town. "Getting the lay of the land. I just moved here, but everyone has already told me how wonderful the library is."

The man preened a bit at that. "Thank you. And it's absolutely true. Not that I'm biased. I'm Liam Reynard-Lowe, the head librarian."

"Riley Henderson, the new musician-in-residence at the big hotel." Riley shook the man's hand.

Liam gave him a head-to-toe once-over that seemed to see down to his bones. "That's you? I heard someone was going to be playing. You met a friend of mine in the grocery store yesterday."

"Brandon? The tall guy? Wow—word travels fast around here." Riley wondered what it meant—if it meant anything at all—that Brandon had mentioned their meeting to a friend.

"You have no idea," Liam said. "It's a town full of psychics, remember? People around here know what you're going to do before you've even done it. But don't let that bother you—unless you're a serial killer." He leaned forward. "You aren't, are you?"

Riley wasn't sure whether to be amused or offended. "No. No. I'm a musician."

Liam nodded with a serious expression. "Good. Welcome to Fox Hollow. Our library is small but mighty. There's a poster with the month's coming events—the next one up is Moose Appreciation Day."

"Seriously?"

"You've got something against moose?" Liam's voice took on an edge.

Riley raised his hands in appeasement. "No. Of course not. I'm sure they're very nice."

Liam gave a curt nod. "You're forgiven."

Riley couldn't tell if the other man was joking or not.

"We've got e-book and audiobook lending programs, there's a display for new books just added, and there are public computers in the back if you need them." Liam continued as if the moose comment hadn't happened.

"There's always a community art display, and we have classes on all kinds of things all the time—the only cost is for materials," Liam added. "Between the e-books and the physical ones, we have a very broad catalog and try to have something for everyone."

"That's great." Riley was still trying to get a read on Liam.

"If you can accept additional gigs, I'd like to find out your rate to play for Moose Day," Liam said. "We're doing moose-related books and art, and I'd also like to do a moose-themed sing-along."

Once again, Riley wasn't sure whether or not he was being pranked, but he decided to risk taking Liam seriously. "That sounds interesting. Do you have a playlist?"

"I'm working on one. The sing-along would probably be an hour. We have a budget for the event, but it's not huge." Liam named an amount, and Riley smiled.

"I can do that. Thank you."

"That's great! We'll make sure you're in all the publicity," Liam told him. "The library does its best to offer a lot of things to do, even in the cold months. So does the Fox Institute."

"I'm going to be taking some classes there." Riley stopped short of explaining the subject. He figured people here believed in psychics—and shifters, if the stories were true—but he wasn't ready to explain his non-gift just yet.

"The Institute does a great job," Liam said enthusiastically. "We work closely with them on community programming. I think you'll like it here."

"I already do," Riley answered. "Everyone's been very friendly."

"Well, if you found the donuts, you're already on the right track," Liam said. "Have you been to the comics store?"

Riley nodded with enthusiasm. "Yes. And I met Madden. That store is going to be a real temptation!"

"Be sure you check out the theater. Most people can get streaming via satellite, but our little movie house runs all kinds of fun stuff, like the *Rocky and Bullwinkle* marathon for Moose Day. Sometimes they do live theater there too. Our high school also puts on some good plays."

Liam handed Riley a flier with upcoming library and community events. "Don't be a stranger! You're welcome to have a look around—just save the donuts until you get outside."

Riley gave him a jaunty salute and did another circle of the library interior, impressed with what was offered. *No wonder everyone speaks so highly of it. They really make a big effort to bring people together.*

He had grown up in Jamestown, near the southwestern New York border. Although Jamestown wasn't a big city by any stretch, it was a good bit larger than Fox Hollow. Despite it being Riley's hometown, he had never quite found a group that he clicked with.

Maybe it was me. It took a while to grow into my skin.

But deep down, Riley knew that wasn't the whole truth. The town welcomed tourists who came for Lake Chautauqua, the college, or sites like the Lucille Ball Museum, but its furniture and manufacturing industries had waned, and Jamestown hadn't quite redefined itself.

He never "fit" there for more reasons than his orientation and struggled to find an audience for his music, although he had very successful gigs in Ithaca and elsewhere. Riley had been thinking about leaving Jamestown even before his ill-fated relationship with Tate, but when that soured and Tate turned abusive, Riley knew he couldn't stay.

Will Fox Hollow be too small—or just right? Would Brandon understand my weird psychic stuff? It seems like a lot of people in town weren't born here. Maybe if things go well with the music, I can make a place for myself. And see if Brandon and I can make something happen.

Riley finished the donuts and his latte after he left the library and headed over to the Fox Institute. The cold wind off the lake made Riley shiver on the short walk despite his parka. He figured he would toughen up if he stayed long enough—and the more he saw of Fox Hollow, the more he hoped he would have that chance.

A large, Victorian building housed the Fox Institute's administrative offices, and Riley guessed it was probably the original facility. Since its founding in the mid-1800s, the Institute had added dorms and more classrooms but kept the architecture reminiscent of its Victorian roots.

He parked in front of the administrative building and followed the signs to Dr. Jeffries's office, pausing nervously for a moment before knocking.

Am I really ready to do this? What if there's something wrong with being a psychic immune?

Riley gathered his courage, and just as he was about to rap at the door, it opened.

"Hi, Riley." Dr. Jeffries answered the door, a man in his forties with dark hair graying at the temples and blue eyes that held a hint of merriment.

"How—"

Dr. Jeffries shrugged. "Psychic." He grinned and tapped his forehead. "Come in and have a seat."

Riley sat in one of the chairs facing the large wooden desk and tried not to look worried. *If I'm a real psychic immune he won't read how nervous I am from my mind, but my body language isn't keeping any secrets.*

"Relax. And welcome. We're very happy you're here. Have you had a chance to look around the town?"

Riley gave him a quick recap, and Dr. Jeffries's smile widened. "So you've met all the 'usual suspects.' That's a good start."

"I don't—"

"You met some great people who are very active in the life of this town," Jeffries replied. "Liam works small miracles at the library. Brandon's one of our first responders as well as being a guide. You'll see a lot of Brenda at the grocery. Sherri's coffee keeps this town running. Dennis Todd and the hotel people are a big part of this town's success. And Jack's donuts make us all very happy."

"I'm especially partial to the donuts," Riley admitted.

"We all are." Jeffries handed Riley a folder from his desk. "You don't have to read everything right now—take it with you, and bring it back tomorrow filled out and signed. It has your course syllabus and some other information that should be helpful, as well as confirming your stipend and the hotel gig."

"What about the research study? How will that work?" Riley had to admit he was more nervous about being a "lab rat" than taking classes.

"True psychic immunes—nils—are rare," Jeffries said. "In some cases, people believe they are immunes when they just have exceptional shielding or some sort of trauma has caused them to bury their gift deep out of fear or shame. In those situations, if the person wants help, we can work with them to open up their natural abilities."

"What about the rest?" Riley didn't think he had any secret trauma, at least not over anything except being gay and the break-up with Tate.

"Those true immunes actually have a gift—it's psychic silence," Jeffries said. "I'm not a telepath. But for those with any measure of that ability, the world is a disturbing, noisy place. It's almost impossible for them to have privacy without learning how to create shields for themselves. They 'overhear' everyone's thoughts, which includes dirty laundry they didn't want to know. Relationships are hard because they hear the momentary irritations that never get spoken."

Riley could only imagine being in a room with dozens of televisions set to different stations, all blaring. "That would be awful."

Jeffries nodded. "If we can figure out how your immunity works, we might be able to reverse engineer something telepaths could learn to cut down on the noise. And if it turns out that you have other gifts underneath the silence, you'll have an option to investigate those as well."

"That sounds great," Riley said. "What is the snow day policy?"

Jeffries laughed. "I guess you've heard everyone talk about the big storms coming in? We probably get more snow and bad weather than what you were used to in Jamestown, but folks here in town cope pretty well.

"Most people and all of the businesses have generators, so the power doesn't stay out for long," Jeffries assured him. "We advise folks to put together a winter emergency kit—there's a list of basic supplies on the town website. You might want to check it and load up on anything you don't already have while you're in town."

"Do places stay open?" Riley asked. Jamestown always seemed to struggle with being overly careful or not careful enough when it came to weather advisories.

"Schools will close for in-person classes if the snow gets too bad—including the Institute—but there's usually an online alternative since we can't just shut down all winter. A lot of folks in these parts have snowmobiles or four-wheel drive vehicles with snow tires, studded tires, and tire chains. We have plows and salt trucks that run all day and all night, if need be," Jeffries replied.

"Not to mention the kind of folks that stay here for the winter are stubborn cusses," he added in a fond tone. "They take precautions and avoid crazy risks, but they have the know-how and equipment to get around on all but the worst days. Businesses might cut hours short, but they'll open if they can. Hell, I've seen food delivery on snowmobiles."

"Wow. That's definitely not how things were back in Jamestown," Riley admitted.

"You'll get used to it if you're meant to be here," Jeffries assured him. "And believe it or not, we have people who come to the Adirondacks for the winter camping experience. It's beautiful, don't get me wrong, but I don't go outside more than I have to when things get bad."

Riley shivered just thinking about it. "I watched a documentary once about Arctic explorers. I think if it were up to me, the North Pole would still be undiscovered."

"Get the right clothes—plenty of layers—and good outerwear and boots, and you might change your mind," Jeffries said. "We have a lot of outdoor fun in the winter—bonfires, snowmobile races with a big indoor/outdoor party afterward, an ice sculpture competition, and lots of ice fishing. Get Brandon to take you on one of his hikes so you can see the territory. This is a beautiful place."

"I think I'm going to like it here," Riley said and meant it. He and Jeffries chatted a few minutes, and then Riley rose to leave.

"I'm playing at the hotel for the first time tonight. If you're free, please show up—I hate playing to an empty room." Riley didn't actually think the room would be completely empty, but he figured it didn't hurt to prime the well.

"I'll get there late, but I wouldn't miss it," Jeffries told him. "And be sure you put a flier up on the bulletin board by the main doors as well as in the library. I sent in your performance schedule to the town activities web site and their Facebook page."

"Thank you. Now if the weather just cooperates," he added nervously.

"Tonight's supposed to be clear and cold. That won't keep anyone away. And it's Wing Night at the hotel bar. That's sort of a holy obligation in these parts."

That went well. I like it here. Scares me a little how "right" it feels, he thought as he was leaving.

Now if I can just get a chance with Brandon…

Anger, fear, and grief might have sent him running to Fox Hollow, but maybe if he stayed long enough, he could heal old wounds.

Riley went back to his room and unpacked more of his things, making sure he set out everything he would need to wear for his gig. He put a box on the bed and opened it, staring at the contents and forcing down bile.

Portable security cameras. Extra locks. A motion detector. Things normal people don't need in their hotel rooms.

"Normal" people don't have stalker exes that might follow them into the wilderness. If I've got evidence, maybe the sheriff won't think I'm imagining things, like the cops back in Jamestown.

His breakup with Tate had been loud and public by design so that everyone knew they weren't together anymore, no matter what story Tate tried to spin.

Tate hadn't taken a swing at Riley, although the regular patrons at their favorite bar seemed primed to expect violence. In public, Tate didn't shout or throw things either. He did his best gaslighting with an audience, playing the confused, wounded, and jilted lover begging for a chance to make things right.

Riley had expected the performance and made it clear—loudly enough for everyone to hear—that he was done being pushed around and controlled. He had stayed cool and rational so that Tate couldn't turn his emotions against him or use them to garner sympathy for himself.

Then again, a psi-vamp would have gotten a feast off the emotions of everyone in that room.

Tate had tried guilting Riley to come back, but when that didn't work and Riley's resolve held firm, Tate switched tactics. He gossiped about Riley to their friends, succeeding in turning a few to his side. Tate love-bombed him with flowers, offered to take him on a luxurious vacation, swore his temper tantrums would never happen again.

Riley hadn't wavered as he put his escape plan in place. Tate must have guessed Riley planned to leave because he upped his game, keying the Pilot's paint, giving him a flat tire, running into his bumper.

Riley had moved out of the apartment he shared with Tate, taking a room at an extended-stay motel until he could sublet a place across town. Despite putting distance between the two of them, Tate managed to show up nearby far more often than coincidence could explain. Most of those times, Tate didn't approach him—he just stood on the other side of the street from wherever Riley had been, staring.

Unsure of the loyalties of their mutual friends and afraid to involve anyone else, Riley kept to himself. He constantly checked for surveillance cameras or tags and found a few, which he destroyed. Riley only went out when he knew Tate would be at work, except for his gigs. Tate made a habit of showing up whenever Riley played, just sitting and staring. Riley paid a bouncer to walk him to his car.

Tate had started off begging and ended up making dark predictions that were ominous even if they weren't legally threats. Riley took the messages as they were meant.

Why did he pick me if I'm really an immune? Whatever psychic manipula-

tion he might have used on other boyfriends probably didn't work on me. Was I a challenge? Or just a handy snack?

Before Riley made the long drive to Fox Hollow, he made an appointment at a garage outside of Jamestown for an inspection to make sure Tate hadn't done anything more dangerous. The mechanic found evidence of tampering and fixed the issues, but Riley couldn't prove Tate had done it.

After that, Riley paused his social media accounts, turned off every tracking app he had, screened all his calls, and changed his emails.

Putting in the removable security cameras gave Riley a little control back and some peace of mind. He put the small devices where they could monitor the door and windows to his room, as well as one over the peephole. For his SUV, the cams went on the dashboard and facing outward to see anyone who approached the car.

At least if Tate tries something, I'll have a witness.

He had alarms for the hotel door and windows, and he kept a personal device in his pocket. Riley hated having to think like a hunted animal, but he had seen a side of Tate that he dared not discount for all the man's charm.

Riley was so deep in his thoughts that he jumped when an email alert chimed. It was from one of the very few friends Riley kept on his contact list, and he weighed whether or not to respond.

Can't hurt to see what he's sent. I don't have to respond.

He opened the email.

Hey Riley! Where've you been? Haven't seen you in a while. Guess you and Tate broke up? He's been asking about you. Don't tell me. I can't blab what I don't know, but I'll miss you. Don't blame you for getting out. Wishing you love and luck. – Caleb

---

Riley realized his hand was shaking. He sat down on the bed and took several deep breaths.

Sooner or later, he's going to find me. I'm a musician. The places I play have to promote my gigs. Even if I'd used a stage name, all it takes is one photo, and he'll find me.

I need to file my restraining order with the sheriff here.

Maybe this is too far away for Tate to bother.

Should I run even farther away? Out west, maybe? But I like it here. I've got a job, and the people are nice. And even if I went to California, Tate could find me if he tries hard enough.

Shit—if Tate's still looking for me, maybe I shouldn't start something with Brandon. I don't want to put him in danger. Tate doesn't love me, but he won't want someone else to, either.

All the good feelings from earlier in the day vanished, leaving Riley despondent. Miserable and scared, he curled up on his bed, set his phone alarm, and hoped he could lose his worries in sleep.

His dreams picked up where Riley's brief encounter with Brandon had left off.

Riley loved how solid Brandon's body felt against him, hard in all the right places. He had never dated someone that much larger, and now he definitely knew it was a kink because Riley felt completely hot and bothered from the first touch.

"Riley," the bigger man whispered, leaning in to kiss. Riley rose on his tip-toes, another new experience, immediately addictive.

Brandon's hands moved from stroking Riley's face to landing on his shoulders. As their kiss deepened, Brandon's grip moved down Riley's arms, then fell to his hips, pulling them together so the press of their hard cocks was unmistakable.

"Want you," Brandon growled, and he grabbed Riley by the ass, lifting him off his feet.

Brandon's kisses swallowed Riley's yelp of surprise. Riley's past lovers had all been close enough to his own height and frame that being picked up as if he weighed nothing sent a thrill through him.

Riley wrapped his legs around Brandon's waist, and Brandon turned them to the wall, pushing Riley's back against it and kneading his ass cheeks as his mouth worked its way from lips to chin and started down Riley's tender neck.

"What do you want?"

"You. Everything," Riley panted. Brandon kissed his way down Riley's throat. Teeth gently nipped where his neck and shoulder joined, and Riley saw

stars. He thought for a moment that Brandon might bite him—and he was surprisingly okay with that.

Instead, Brandon sucked a hickey where it wouldn't show, but Riley would feel and see it for days.

"Mine," Brandon whispered. "Mate."

"Yours." Riley was sure he was about to cream his jeans like a teenager between the friction of their clothed thrusts and how hot it was that Brandon took the lead.

"Mate," Riley groaned as he felt his climax build. "Only you."

Brandon growled as he ground against Riley, and both of them arched as their orgasms hit, making Riley writhe in Brandon's arms, pinned between his strong body and the wall. The hickey pulsed on his neck, a delicious ache, and he hoped it would mark him for days.

Riley woke moaning Brandon's name, wet and sticky in his jeans. The dream seemed so real. He touched his face where Brandon's fingers had ghosted down his skin and felt for the spot on his neck where the hickey had been.

He wished that by some psychic miracle he would see the marks of their passion when he took off his shirt, already sad to think it was only a dream.

Mate?

Riley frowned, puzzled. "Mine" he understood and wished with all his heart it was true.

But mate?

And I said it back to him. Who does that?

One incredible possibility presented itself. *Shifters?*

Riley had read his share of shifter romance and fan fiction. In the stories there were claiming bites and fated mates. *I think we're safe from MPreg.*

Could Brandon be a shifter?

They said Fox Hollow is a haven for shifters as well as psychics. And if shifters are real, maybe they can recognize each other. So anyone who doesn't spot them—isn't in the club.

If Brandon is a shifter, will me being a nil matter since I don't have a furry alter-ego?

Would he even be interested in someone who is just human—and unread-able for psychics as well?

He thought about the people he had met in town and how his mind helpfully supplied what they might look like as talking animals in a Disney cartoon. Madden definitely gave off squirrel vibes. Sherri at the café had made him think of a brown bear.

If it's true about shifters in Fox Hollow, it makes sense there would be a lot of them around.

If Brandon is a shifter, what would he be? He's big. A deer, maybe?

Imagining his crush as a white-tailed buck made Riley snicker.

One step at a time. Before I get to find out about his "tail" I need to ask him out on a date. Let's see if he shows up at one of my gigs.

Riley hadn't dared date while he was still in Jamestown after he and Tate broke up. The hurt was too new, and the danger too great.

But with time, distance, and the chance of a fresh start, Riley knew he could find the courage to try again—with the right guy.

His alarm went off, breaking off his musings and reminding him that it was time to get ready for his big night.

The hotel agreed to store his amps in a secure place, so that meant Riley just had to move his instruments. He showered and shaved, taking care to pick out a blue shirt that played up his eyes and tight jeans that left nothing to the imagination. After a moment of dithering over footwear, he figured his Timberlands would fit right in—and keep him from falling on his ass in the snow.

If Brandon shows up, I hope he likes what he sees.

A flutter of excitement tingled through him.

I hope things work out here. I haven't felt this good—this much like the old me—in a long time.

Riley carried two guitars out to his SUV—an electric one and an acoustic. That gave him flexibility with the song choices. For his first night, he planned to stick with his set list, but if the crowd was friendly and the night went well, he hoped to add requests to later evenings.

Dennis Todd met him at the back door with another man, one close to Riley's own age. "This is Tyler—he's one of the hotel's owners. He's on duty tonight, but I wanted to handle the introductions."

Tyler and Riley shook hands. "You need a hand with anything?"

Riley shook his head. "Not tonight. I didn't bring my keyboard. Thought I'd keep it simple this time." He had plenty of practice wending his way through the back corridors of hotels with a guitar case in each hand and a backpack for his set list, picks, and spare strings.

"The room is filling up," Tyler said as Riley followed him through the maze of passageways. "I think you're going to have an enthusiastic crowd."

Tyler moved with unusual grace, like a big cat. *Shifter?* Riley wondered. Now that the thought had crossed his mind, he kept trying to match people with possible animal counterparts.

A round of applause greeted Riley when he walked on stage. His setup on the bar stage left room for patrons at the regular tables but made him more visible to the folks in the back.

"Hi everyone, I'm Riley." He leaned into the mike as he got his guitar ready and checked the connections. "Thanks for coming out tonight. We're going to have fun."

Once his eyes got used to the lighting, he scanned the room as he sound checked his guitar. Brandon hadn't showed up, and Riley felt a pang of disappointment.

He might have to work. Maybe he was giving me time to warm up. It doesn't mean anything.

Unless it does.

Riley's nervousness slipped away after a few songs, some of his favorites intentionally put first as an ice breaker for himself and the audience. Their warm response encouraged him, and he began to enjoy the music.

Whenever he played a new location, Riley planned a playlist of pop favorites, mostly upbeat, with a few slower or faster songs for contrast. Being in a bar or restaurant meant he wasn't the star attraction and could still expect people to chat and eat while he was performing. Once he got to know a crowd, he would work in some of his own songs when they fit the mood.

As the evening wore on, if he picked the right songs, the audience's attention would shift from their after-dinner drinks to listening to the music. Riley knew he had to earn a following here and paid attention to which songs had people swaying and mouthing the words and when they went back to quietly chatting.

For the most part, he had the audience on board, and Riley felt pleased. Toward the end of his first set, Brandon slipped in and took a seat at the bar.

Riley felt a flush of heat on the back of his neck remembering his explicit dream, and shifted on his chair as his body responded. Brandon made eye contact and nodded with encouragement, then closed his eyes and seemed to lose himself in the songs, leaving his beer untouched.

"I'm going to take a little break, but I'll be back real soon," Riley said when he finished a song. The applause felt sincere, not forced, and he grinned, setting down his guitar and leaving the stage. He headed straight for Brandon.

Brandon flashed a wide smile and indicated the bar stool next to him. "Great songs. I loved your playlist."

"Thanks." Riley was pleased at the praise and Brandon's obvious interest.

"Can I buy you a beer? Or a soda if you can't drink when you're playing?" Brandon asked.

"A Coke would be great, thanks," Riley answered, and Brandon signaled the bartender.

"Have you gotten settled yet?" Brandon toyed with the paper coaster under his drink.

Maybe he's a little nervous too.

"I didn't bring much with me, so it didn't take long," Riley joked. "The room is nice, and it has everything I need. I went over to the Institute and got my paperwork, although my classes don't start for another week."

Brandon looked like he wanted to say something and thought better of it. *Maybe he's wondering what I'm going to study and doesn't want to pry.*

"How about you?" Riley wanted to keep the conversation going as long as his short break allowed.

"I'm taking a group out on a hike tomorrow. We'll be back before the big storm, but if you don't see me around—or see me here—that's why," Brandon said, and Riley melted a little that he had thought to explain his absence.

"I'm glad you came tonight. I hope I didn't make your ears bleed," Riley joked.

"You have a beautiful voice." Brandon's hand brushed against Riley's, and he held eye contact. Brandon shifted on his stool, turning toward Riley, and their knees pressed against each other. "I enjoyed listening to your videos online."

I'm not imagining it. He's interested. Holy fuck!

Riley hoped he wasn't grinning like a fool. His pulse raced, and his hands felt sweaty like he was asking out his first high school crush.

"Thank you. I try to pick songs that fit my range."

"How did you get into music?" Brandon leaned one elbow on the bar but turned to face Riley. Between the angle of his broad shoulders and his long legs, he carved out a private space for them.

"My mom played the piano, so I learned that first. I picked up guitar in high school and stuck with it. Started playing with bands and in bars as soon as they'd let me," Riley remembered. "When I'm doing a place like this, I mostly stick to covers of famous songs, but in my spare time, I like to try my hand at writing some."

"I'd love to hear them—if you'd play for me." Brandon's dark eyes met Riley's, and Riley thought he'd melt on the spot.

"I'd like that." Riley liked having Brandon's full attention and being the focus of his warm smile. "Oh, I forgot to mention—I went to the library and talked with Liam. He asked me to play for the moose festival. I'll have to learn the list of songs, but it sounds like a lot of fun."

"I'm sure the moose will appreciate it," Brandon teased. Riley had the oddest feeling that he had missed something, but he smiled anyhow.

"I'm impressed by how much goes on here. I was afraid everyone hibernated."

"Well, some folks try their hardest," Brandon replied. Once again, Riley felt like there was a subtext he was missing, but that thought flew out of his mind when their knees bumped.

"If you've got a little time before your classes start, I'd like to take you out for dinner. Our restaurants aren't fancy, but the food is awesome," Brandon offered.

"That would be great. I'd like that." Riley hoped he didn't sound too eager, but he had never believed in playing hard-to-get when he saw someone he wanted.

He suddenly couldn't think of what to say to keep the conversation going. A tent card on the table advertised *Zodiac Bingo*.

"What's your sign?" Riley blurted. "I'm a Gemini."

Brandon looked quizzical for a moment, then saw the tent card and caught up. "Aries." A slow smile spread across his face. "Perfect pairing. Maybe it's written in the stars."

Riley felt himself blush, which was so not his usual reaction. "I like the sound of that." His watch beeped.

"Oops—need to go back for the second set. Maybe we can pick a day after you get back?"

Brandon grinned. "Definitely. Now go knock our socks off."

Riley returned to the stage, greeted by a smattering of applause. He picked up his guitar and strummed it, mentally running through his playlist.

He didn't want to scare Brandon off or lose the audience with songs that were too sappy, but sharing his heart through his music came naturally. Riley rearranged a few selections to highlight songs about crushes, love at first sight, meeting someone special, and moved those up in his set, filling in feel-good favorites in between.

I'd like to send a message but not come on too strong. Does Brandon have any psychic ability? If so, what does he sense from me?

Maybe we'll need a conversation about that…but not yet.

I'm overthinking this. We're both interested. That's a good start.

Riley's second set flew by. The audience clapped along and swayed to the music now that their meals were finished and they lingered over drinks. The room wasn't full, but it wasn't a bad crowd for a Friday night and his first time there.

He preferred a lighter crowd than a packed house until he could judge how this audience reacted to his song choices. Given that it wasn't tourist season, Riley figured these were local regulars, and he wanted to give them a great night so they would come back often.

Brandon stayed for the whole second set. When the bar closed, and everyone else drifted out, Brandon walked forward to where Riley broke down his equipment.

"You've got a lot of stuff. Need a hand?" Brandon offered.

Riley looked up and flashed a grateful smile. "Sure. I'll never turn down help. The good thing is that the amps and heavy things are staying here, so I don't have to carry them back and forth. That means it's just my guitar cases."

"One for you, one for me. That works," Brandon replied.

One of the hotel's tech staff checked with Riley to make sure everything had gone smoothly and then began unplugging and winding the cords.

Riley nestled his guitars in their velvet-lined cases and tucked the other things he used in his set into his backpack, which he managed to shoulder over his coat.

"Ready?"

Brandon already wore his parka and had an adorable knit beanie with an embroidered moose.

"Lead on."

Riley stopped by the bar and found Brandon had already paid for his soda.

"When you're not working, I'll take you out for a real drink," Brandon joked.

"See you tomorrow night, Riley," Connor, the bartender replied with a wave. "You had a good crowd for a first time. I think you'll do real well here."

Brandon set the guitar into the back of the Pilot, next to where Riley placed the other case. "Do you have snow tires? You're going to need them here."

Riley warmed at the concern. "Bought a set right before I came, and I've got chains and sand in the back."

"Good. They do their best to keep up with the roads, but a heavy snowfall makes it tough, and black ice is always a danger. Please be careful." Brandon hesitated like he wanted to lean in and steal a kiss.

Riley froze, not sure what to do, wanting to stretch up and meet Brandon's lips but afraid of misreading the signals.

The moment passed, and Brandon clapped him on the shoulder. "I'll see you when I get back from the trail tour. Stay warm, and knock 'em dead in the bar."

"Be safe," Riley managed, tongue-tied.

Riley watched Brandon walk away, still kicking himself for not seizing the moment.

We're going on a date. There'll be other chances. I really think he's interested.

Now I just have to keep from screwing it up.

Riley waited in his SUV for a moment when he got back to the motel before he got out, cautiously scanning the parking lot. When he didn't spot a threat, he grabbed his guitars and hurried to his door, disarming the portable alarm. He slipped inside, reset the alarm, and locked the door, including the extra lock he had brought with him.

Out of habit, Riley paused in the doorway once the lights were on to scan the room, assuring himself nothing was out of place.

How long am I going to feel like this? I don't want to be twitchy around Brandon. If we get together, he'll hear my whole sad story soon enough—I'd like to have some time when he doesn't know that part of my history.

Riley went to the window and peeked outside. Moonlight lit the snow, making even the parking lot look magical.

Something moved at the edge of the trees, and Riley went on alert. A large, dark form stepped from beneath the pines, and Riley caught his breath.

"A moose. That's a real moose."

The handsome creature moved farther into the moonlight, just enough that Riley could make out its height, the muscular body, and the broad rack of antlers.

"He's beautiful," Riley whispered.

The moose seemed to make eye contact for a moment, and Riley felt safe, like the moose, impossibly, was his protector.

Seconds later, the moose walked into the woods as if he owned them.

I hope he comes back. I like knowing he's out there, watching over me.

Not that the moose thinks that, but I can pretend.

Riley yawned, remembering that it was late. Playing usually energized him, but with all the changes in his life and the effort of navigating a new town, he felt exhausted.

He got ready for bed, walked the perimeter of his room checking the security equipment, and took a moment to assure himself that nothing worrisome had turned up on the cameras while he was gone.

Riley fell into bed, still glowing about seeing Brandon at the bar. He fell asleep happy, thinking of his date with Brandon and the "guardian" moose he had spotted. For the first time in a long while, Riley slept soundly without bad dreams.

$$5$$

BRANDON

As happy as Brandon had been to fit in one more tour before the storms came, he chafed at the delay it caused in getting to know Riley better.

His clients remarked on the scenery, joked and teased as they fished out on the ice, and huddled around the campfire in the evening to tell stories and talk about what they had seen. Brandon tried to be engaging and draw them out, but his mind was back in Fox Hollow despite his best efforts.

Riley's singing stirred something deep in Brandon's heart, and he suspected a mate bond had something to do with the feelings that surged bright and hot after only a brief acquaintance.

We should be back with our mate, getting to know him better, Brandon's inner moose nudged.

We need to eat. I have to work to buy food.

We can graze the trees for free, his moose argued.

Pine needles get stuck in my throat.

Humans are too fragile. That's why moose are better, his other half snarked. Brandon ignored the razzing, long a part of their rapport.

I don't think Riley is a shifter. So wooing our mate is going to be strictly human. Lucky you have me.

He's very handsome. Bite him and claim him before someone else does.

I'm not taking dating advice from a moose.

You need to take it from someone. We've been alone too long.

Brandon sighed, watching his clients enjoying a snowball fight. *True. But something is odd. I couldn't read him at all last night, even when we were in contact. Usually, when someone gets that close, I'm overwhelmed keeping their thoughts out of my head. I sensed…warm feelings…but not words.*

He hasn't said what he's studying, and I don't want to pry—but I'm really curious. If he really is a psychic immune, we're going to need to do a lot of talking instead of relying on my telepathy. What does that mean for a mate bond?

Brandon tried to bring his attention back to the moment, telling himself there was plenty of time to find answers. His clients were a jovial group who knew each other well, which meant Brandon didn't have to play host to warm up the connections. He chimed in occasionally, but they clearly had a history and in-jokes, so he took the opportunity to stay more detached and focus on the forest.

For what it's worth, we're the perfect zodiac match. I intend to take that as a good omen.

Brandon obsessively checked the weather, unwilling to risk his charges in the woods when a storm hit. The storms were predicted to be a few days out, but he noticed that the sky had grown darker and the temperature dropped.

He made the decision to change their route, something his clients wouldn't notice but which would keep them closer to civilization, making it faster if they needed to go back to town in a hurry. Forecasts were all well and good, but Brandon had been a guide long enough to know that they weren't perfect and a dangerous storm could move in more quickly than expected.

Brandon relied on his moose more than any weather app. The longer they were outside, the more he felt certain that the snow would hit sooner than predicted. They were well-provisioned for a normal day, but not to face down a major squall.

He was glad to have altered the route when snow began falling, light at first and then heavier as the afternoon wore on.

"The storm is ahead of projections," he told his disappointed clients. "We need to head back now. We don't want to get stranded out here. I know it's a day sooner than we planned, and I'll give you all a day's credit for another hike."

To his surprise, the group accepted his decision with only minor disappointment. Then again, the slate-gray sky and accumulating snow proved Brandon's point, and this set of hikers seemed less risk-prone than others he had led.

Sometimes he got a group that viewed hiking like a video game with challenges but not real risks. That meant he had to be on watch constantly to keep them from accidentally hurting themselves or endangering the whole group.

Fortunately, both regular animals and shifters could sense Brandon's moose-ness and didn't want to mess with a full-grown buck.

Because we're badass, his moose chimed in.

I'd just as soon not test that in a fight. Brandon had no desire for a scuffle, but in general, a moose was likely to win any match except against a bear or a pack of wolves.

The snow fell harder as they retraced their steps, confirming Brandon's caution. Over the last couple of hours, several inches had fallen, and if the revised forecast held true, they could expect a few feet by the time it passed.

"Does this happen a lot around here?" one of his clients asked, looking windburned and cold.

"More often than not." Brandon trudged in front to plow the path for the others. His long legs made even deep snow easier to navigate. With snowshoes, he could go nearly anywhere in his human form that his moose could go.

"How do you manage?" another spoke up, his face nearly covered by his hat and scarf.

"We learn to read the signs, regardless of what the forecast says," Brandon replied. "Satellites and predictions are great, but sometimes they're wrong. That's cold comfort if you're stuck out in the elements." He didn't mention that his moose had a strong natural instinct for storms.

"Do people get lost out here?" another hiker asked from the back of the group.

"Unfortunately, yes. This forest is especially rugged, and between the weather and the terrain, it can be dangerous if you don't know what you're doing," Brandon said. "Every year people get injured because they go off a trail and fall or get lost. Most turn out okay, but some people are never found."

"I thought this was a state park," one of the hikers questioned, looking sodden and tired.

"It is—but it's not a theme park," Brandon replied. "It's still 'forever wild.' There aren't safety precautions built in except for the knowledge and equipment you bring with you."

Brandon sighed in relief when they reached the parking lot, although they still had to navigate the roads back to town. They loaded their gear and piled into his Suburban. Brandon felt pleased and relieved that the group bantered in high spirits, commenting on the highlights of what they had seen.

When they got back to Fox Hollow, he drove them to the hotel and issued their vouchers. "I'd love to take you back out in another season so you can see how different it can be," he offered. "Summer and fall are especially nice here."

The good mood of the majority seemed to rub off on the one hiker who had been most disappointed about cutting the excursion short, and Brandon let out a sigh of relief when they gathered their equipment and trundled into the hotel.

Brandon waved goodbye and checked the time. If he hurried, he could go home, unpack, and still be back to eat dinner at the hotel bar and catch Riley's set. After a full day of hiking, he couldn't promise to last until the end of the evening, but the thought of getting a little time together perked him up from the disappointing outing.

Snow that cut the excursion short didn't bother the people in town. Plows and salt trucks cycled through the streets, and Brandon's SUV could handle the weather.

He found a spot at the bar and ordered dinner. The cold and the exertion had given him quite an appetite, and despite his moose's prodding to strip leaves and twigs in the woods, Brandon was much more in the mood for a cheeseburger and fries.

We weren't really going to be in any danger. Worst case we could have hauled them all out on a sledge.

I have no desire to cause a panic or attract the wrong kind of attention, Brandon reminded his other half. *Museums still stuff and display moose, you know—especially maybe a moose shifter who gets caught on camera.*

Barbaric. When have moose ever done the same to people?

Taxidermy is tough with hooves instead of hands.

That's not the point.

The idea of shifting had occurred to Brandon in case of an extreme emergency. Still, he didn't want to end up on social media even though Fox Hollow had a long reputation as a home for shifters. People who might believe that the psychics at the Institute were real often just smiled and nodded at the idea of shifters. Brandon knew that the unrealistic depiction in television shows and movies didn't help encourage acceptance of the real thing. Whether the denial was good or bad remained up for debate.

No one wanted to end up conscripted into a secret government project. Brandon had seen enough movies to know that never ended well. He suspected that the witches that were part of the Institute played a part in keeping the town from gaining the wrong kind of notice.

"I didn't think you'd be back yet." Riley took the stool next to his, and Brandon noticed that the other man managed to move his seat a few inches closer than it had been.

"Couldn't stay away," Brandon joked, twitching his fingers just enough to stroke Riley's hand.

Riley gave a coy smile in return. "I like the sound of that."

Brandon sighed. "It's true—and being here tonight is a benefit. The sky looked bad. I think the storm is going to hit sooner than we originally thought. Didn't want a bunch of less experienced hikers out in the wild if that happened."

"Makes sense. I bet you're a good guide."

"When the weather breaks, I'd love to show you my favorite places," Brandon offered. "They don't all need a big hike to get to.

There's a lot of beautiful scenery and some spots other people overlook."

"That sounds really good." Riley's fingers slid close and stayed touching Brandon's hand.

"Haven't forgotten that dinner invitation either," Brandon said. "Just as soon as the weather breaks."

Riley met his gaze. Brandon wanted to believe he read the same interest—and lust—that he felt. He hoped that was the case. Much as Brandon knew it was best to take things slow, especially since he didn't know much about Riley's past, his cock had other ideas.

Mate, his moose nudged. *You'll always be in rut for your true mate.*

I am not in rut.

Whatever you want to tell yourself, his moose dismissed.

"I'd like to see all your favorite places." Riley dropped his voice to a lower pitch that sent blood straight to Brandon's groin. "Do you ever do private tours?"

"Only for very special people." It had been so long since Brandon had flirted, he feared he was hopelessly out of practice. He admired Riley's easy confidence and lightheartedness. Brandon knew he could be moody and fearful of failure, but if the horoscopes were right, a Gemini lover would add balance and fun. He would have pursued Riley regardless of his sign, but knowing they were a perfect zodiac match boosted his confidence.

They ordered burgers, and after the server left, Riley still studied the menu.

"I'm sort of surprised that for a wilderness kind of place, there isn't more exotic stuff on the menu," Riley observed. "Like venison—or local fish."

Brandon fought the urge to heave. Most people thought of deer when they mentioned venison, but it could also mean elk or moose.

"I'm not a fan," he said, not wanting to throw up on his crush. "Doesn't set well with me."

"Just curious."

"I don't think you'd like it," Brandon said hurriedly. "Too gamey and tough."

I bet you wouldn't say that if he wanted to suck on your meatstick, his moose prompted.

Don't be crude.

Get him to come home with you and impress him with your sizeable… rack.

If you ever want that to happen, go away.

Fussy one, aren't you? his other half grumped, but he retreated in Brandon's mind.

"I guess I can see not wanting to eat wild game if you're a guide," Riley said.

Without Riley understanding about the shifters, Brandon couldn't explain that game meat was strictly off the menu in Fox Hollow. Livestock was a safer source, avoiding tragic hunting mistakes or issues around cannibalism. Elsewhere in the Adirondacks, hunting was both big business and a popular hobby. But it was banned within a ten-mile radius around Fox Hollow for the safety of both the shifters and the hunters.

Brandon nodded. "I'm much more into photography."

"There are plenty of great things to take pictures of around here," Riley replied. "I've never been one for hunting either."

Thank heavens.

"Oh—I wanted to tell you. I saw a real moose! It was at the edge of the woods outside my motel room," Riley said excitedly. "I only saw the silhouette, but it was absolutely…majestic."

"Oh yeah?" Brandon tried not to preen.

"I never realized how big they are," Riley went on. "Just huge. I was expecting something more like deer. I saw those in a petting zoo I went to as a kid."

Brandon snorted. "I don't think you'll find moose in a petting zoo."

"The antlers alone are massive," Riley gushed. "And it was so tall."

"Keep an eye out. You might see him again."

"He looked like something out of a legend." Riley sounded smitten.

He thinks we're handsome. Did you hear that?

Except he doesn't know it was us.

Still, it's a good omen for when he finds out. He will swoon over our mooseness and fall madly in love.

Get over yourself.

"I was wondering—is it true that there are shifters in Fox Hollow?"

Brandon barely avoided choking. "Why do you ask?"

To Riley's credit, he didn't dismiss the idea out of hand. "Jeffries said this was a haven for psychics and shifters, and psychics are real, so why not shifters? Have you ever met one?"

"Probably. I doubt a shifter would announce it unless they trusted someone," Brandon sidestepped. He glanced around the bar. Half the people there were shifters, and the others were with the Institute. Fox Hollow discouraged year-round residents without supernatural abilities. Having a witch nudge a prospect's interests to the next town might strain real estate ethics, but the townsfolk had too much at risk to let "mundanes" settle permanently, although tourists were always welcome.

"Are you looking forward to your classes at the Institute?" Brandon hoped Riley would offer a clue about the subject. Try as he might, Brandon couldn't read him, feeding his suspicions that whatever Riley was studying had something to do with his unusually quiet thoughts.

"I guess. Trying to figure out if something is a talent or a deficiency." Riley looked down.

"Every superpower has its pluses and minuses." Brandon intentionally tried to lighten the mood. He had the feeling that Riley felt conflicted about whatever brought him to the Institute.

"I guess you're right. I'm just so impressed with the idea that some people can read minds or see the future. That seems so...useful."

Brandon moved his hand to slide along Riley's. "I guess it all depends. Abilities don't have to be like in the movies to be powerful. Sometimes small gifts can have a big impact."

"I guess I'll learn all about that," Riley replied. "People here are very laid back about the whole thing."

"You're new in town. Once people get to know you, they'll open up," Brandon replied. "They just need to trust you."

Riley met his gaze. "What about you? Bend any spoons? Raise the dead? Light candles without a match?"

Brandon looked away, trying to figure out how to answer without lying in a way that didn't scare Riley off. "I hear thoughts." He decided that if the truth came between them, then there had never been any chance of connecting.

"Seriously? Like a mind-reader?" Riley seemed curious, not frightened.

"I try very hard not to hear people," Brandon said. "I don't go around eavesdropping. Actually, most of the time, it's difficult to screen people out because it's like everyone is a radio, and they're all playing at full volume. It's noisy."

"What about me?" Riley raised his gaze to meet Brandon's, and Brandon felt something shift between them. "What do you read from me?"

"Nothing. I mean, nothing beyond what non-psychic people can pick up just from body language. So your deep, dark secrets are safe." Brandon hoped he didn't scare Riley away.

"Nothing at all?" Riley pressed, and his intensity made Brandon curious.

Brandon concentrated, and chanced laying his hand over Riley's. Physical contact usually strengthened a psychic connection. Brandon picked up more of Riley's feelings but not his thoughts.

"I can get a little of your emotions, but not what you're thinking," Brandon said. "Please don't be weirded out. I don't go around listening in if I can help it. People deserve privacy and there's a whole lot of stuff I just don't want to know."

"What am I feeling right now?" Riley had a glint in his eyes.

Brandon took a chance and held his hand. Riley didn't pull away. "You're curious. And you're not afraid." He stared at Riley, wondering if the other man could read his hope and vulnerability even without being psychic. "But not words or actual thoughts. Just surface feelings."

Riley nodded. "I'm a nil. At least, that's what I've been told. Dr. Jeffries says we're rare, and he's going to do a study with me. It's not something I can control—at least, not as far as I know," he dropped his gaze. "I hope that's not a bad thing."

Brandon squeezed his hand. "No, not bad at all. Thank you for telling me. I suspected, but I didn't know for sure—because I can't read you much. And don't apologize…it's kind of peaceful."

"Really?"

Brandon nodded. "People are noisy. It's distracting. Some think so loud it's very hard *not* to overhear. I've had to spend years learning how to screen them out—for their sake and mine."

Riley seemed to be taking the confession very well, Brandon thought. He wondered if the other man would accept his moose as easily.

"I can see that. Thank you for telling me." Riley paused. "I'm going to think real hard at you. Tell me if you can figure it out."

He leaned forward on his elbows and stared into Brandon's eyes with a glint of mischief. "What am I thinking now?"

Brandon shut his eyes and concentrated. He didn't see images, but his heightened sense of smell picked up a shift in pheromones, and his cock twitched in response. Everything about Riley's body language and voice signaled attraction and flirting.

"I think you might be in favor of getting to know each other better." Brandon grinned as he opened his eyes.

"And here you didn't think you could read me," Riley teased with a coy smile.

"I'd like that," Brandon admitted and held his breath. He didn't think Riley was toying with him, but he braced for rejection.

"I would too." Riley stroked Brandon's fingers. "Maybe we can get snowed in together. Then we'd have to conserve body heat."

"Hmm…sounds fun even if we're not snowbound," Brandon replied.

Riley's phone chimed. "Time for me to go entertain the crowd. Can you stay?"

"For the first set. I was up really early with the tour, and we came back in deep snow. How about we go to the Moose Festival together? You're playing there, right?"

"Only for an hour. And I hear there's food."

Brandon rolled his eyes. "They rename a lot of snacks to be moose-ish. But it's fun. And I'm reading a couple of children's stories and giving a short presentation on moose. Otherwise, we can wander—and I'll buy dinner afterward."

"It's a date." Riley let his fingertips trail along the back of Brandon's hand before he left to go to the stage. Brandon smelled Riley's intoxicating scent and felt his body react regardless of how tired he was.

Brandon smiled, hoping Riley could read his interest and attraction. "Knock 'em dead out there."

Much as he enjoyed Riley's singing, Brandon felt himself fading after the first set. He stayed just long enough to say goodnight to Riley, who walked him out to his SUV.

"Do you have a safe way back to the motel?" The Lake Motel was only a mile away, but even that could seem like a formidable distance in bad weather.

Riley nodded. "Mr. Todd said that if it got bad, he'd let me stay here. How far do you have to go?"

"My cabin is pretty close. I'll be fine." Brandon wasn't worried about his SUV making it through the snow, and in a pinch, he could trek since he had skis with him.

"Rest up. We've got the Moose Festival coming up," Riley told him, moving closer. He stretched up on his toes and pressed a kiss to Brandon's lips.

"For luck." Riley winked and tossed a glance over his shoulder before he hurried back inside.

Brandon smiled and touched his fingertips to his lips.

Mate, his moose cheered. *Told you so.*

By the time Brandon got to his cabin, the wind sent snow in drifts across the road and several more inches had fallen. He got a fire going in the fireplace and checked the generator, bringing an ample load of wood inside for the night. Clapping his mittened hands together didn't restore feeling in his numbed fingers, so he hurried his preparations.

Brandon unloaded anything that would be damaged by the cold and parked the SUV in the detached garage. He stomped the snow from his boots as he went inside, and the wind erased his prints in seconds.

He changed into comfortable sweats and warm socks and made himself a cup of hot chocolate and some popcorn. As tired as Brandon felt, he wasn't quite relaxed enough to go to bed.

His phone chimed as he settled on the couch, a number he didn't recognize. "Hello?"

"Did you get home safely? I was worried," Riley asked.

Brandon smiled, feeling warm inside that his crush cared. "Just now. Please tell me you're staying at the hotel. It's bad out there."

"I'm staying here. The second set ended early because people wanted to get home. I think even the hotel emergency staff are staying overnight."

"That's good. It's not worth getting in a wreck—or stranded. Thanks for being safe." Brandon was surprised at how much he already cared for Riley and had to agree with his moose about them being mates.

I told you so.

Brandon ignored his other half's snark. "Do you have everything you need if you can't get out for a couple of days?"

"I stuck a spare outfit in my car, just in case. I've got e-books and, if the power goes out and I can't recharge, some paperbacks. Or I can sleep. At least I won't go hungry," Riley replied. "How about you?"

"I stocked up, so I'll be fine," Brandon replied. "Not my first snow-mageddon."

"Sleep tight," Riley said. "And now you have my number."

"Stay warm." Brandon already saved Riley's information as a contact. He sighed when they ended the call. It surprised him how much he missed Riley even though they had just seen each other a few hours ago.

He's our mate. Of course we miss him.

Yeah, but how do I explain that to him? He's not a moose.

Mixed matings are hard. He's attracted to you. That's a good thing.

It would be better if the snow wasn't being a cock-blocker.

True mates find a way.

Brandon flipped channels as he ate his popcorn and sipped hot chocolate with a shot of Kahlua, letting the tension from the day drain away.

All things considered, it was good. I made the right call about ending the tour early, and no one seemed too upset about it. Got to see Riley—and he kissed me. So, I'm not imagining that he's interested. And we have a date—if we get a break in the weather.

His phone buzzed a few moments after he got into bed, with a call from Riley.

"What are you wearing?" Riley asked, and Brandon chuckled.

"Boxer briefs," Brandon replied. "How about you?" His moose always ran hot.

"A T-shirt and flannel pajama pants—and I'm still cold," Riley replied. "Any ideas on how to warm up?"

That was an invitation if Brandon ever heard one. "I can think of a few. Did you have anything in mind?"

"I've heard that sharing body heat can keep someone from freezing to death. I'd hate to get hypothermia."

"Hmm, that wouldn't be good," Brandon returned. "You don't want to get frostbite in sensitive areas."

"I'd like to warm up your sensitive areas," Riley said.

"What are you doing?"

"Touching myself. But I'd rather be touching you."

Brandon felt himself harden. He hadn't expected this from Riley, not this soon anyhow, but he wasn't going to object.

"I'd rather you be touching me too. And I'd like to warm you up all over."

"Mmm," Riley returned. "That sounds like a great idea. We should have stayed together tonight. To ward off hypothermia."

"Exactly."

"Tell me what you like." Brandon imagined Riley lying in his bed, pants shoved down, stroking himself.

"A firm grip…smooth stroke top to bottom…don't forget the balls."

Brandon did his best to hold the phone with his left hand while he slicked his right and began working himself.

"I wouldn't forget them. But I'd suck you first."

Brandon had to grip the base of his cock to keep from coming too soon. "Yeah. Sounds real good."

"Are you close already?"

Brandon was too horny to be embarrassed. It had been too long since he'd had a partner in bed, and even if Riley was long-distance, he was not a figment of Brandon's imagination. "Yeah. Been a while. You?"

"Close. Same. Wish we were together."

"Me too."

"After we go out for dinner, come back to my room with me. We can do this all over again." Riley's invitation and the mental picture it raised in Brandon's mind, pushed him over the edge, and he pumped his come over his fist with a groan.

"Come for me," Brandon murmured.

"Already did. Damn."

Brandon grabbed a tissue and wiped his hand, then fell back onto the bed. "This would be better in person."

"Thinking the same thing. But I couldn't wait."

"Glad you didn't," Brandon replied.

"Sleep tight. See you soon," Riley answered.

"You too."

Brandon lay still for a few minutes, blissed out. *I just had phone sex with Riley.*

That was not sex. Have you forgotten how? his moose countered.

It was definitely a good start. Phone sex wasn't something Brandon had done often, but with Riley, the reluctance melted away.

We could shift and walk back to town. Then we wouldn't be alone.

Let's not surprise him with our mooseness just yet. Don't want to freak him out.

Humans freak out easily, his moose said. *Our mooseness is magnificent.*

Brandon chuckled as his moose retreated to the back of his mind in a snit. *I'm glad he's interested and thinking about getting together. I'm willing to take it slow and make it last. If he's really our mate, that will be okay.*

His moose chuffed. *Fine.*

6
___

RILEY

"The festival is charming. And they do something similar for other types of forest animals too?" Riley asked as he and Brandon walked through the art displays in the library foyer. "You did a great job with the reading."

Brandon blushed a little, which Riley thought was adorable. "Glad you enjoyed it. The kids really like the stories, and it's fun to make them laugh."

"You did a great moose voice," Riley told him.

Brandon started coughing and held up a hand. "I'm okay. Just swallowed wrong."

Phone sex the previous night seemed to shift things between them, breaking the ice and making both men more comfortable with physical contact. Holding hands outside didn't really work with gloves and mittens, but they walked close enough that their shoulders bumped, and at the diner, their knees touched beneath the table, and fingers brushed at every pretext.

Riley's horoscope confirmed what he already knew—that he particularly liked being touched on the arms, throat, and neck and enjoyed sharing a good conversation. So far, Brandon was naturally checking off all the boxes.

"I think this is the best meatloaf I've ever eaten." Riley wiped his mouth and looked at his empty plate. "Is everything on the menu that good?"

Brandon nodded. "Yeah, and the place is always busy, so I'm not the only one who agrees."

"I'd plump up like a hibernating bear if I ate like this all the time," Riley admitted.

"That's the beauty of winter sports. Works off all that good food." Brandon's bright smile made Riley's heart race.

"I plan to take you up on that offer to teach me to cross-country ski. I don't think I'd dare try downhill, but I can shuffle my feet on flat ground with the best of them."

Brandon laughed. "There's a little more to it, but you've got the main idea. Our trails are kept in good shape year-round, so there are safe places to go without worrying about getting lost. And you're not the only one who doesn't want to go flying down the side of a mountain."

After dinner, they headed to the theater to catch part of the Bull-winkle marathon. Despite a great meal and dessert, they both had room for popcorn and soda. Riley picked seats in the back row where they could hold hands and sneak a few kisses like teenagers.

No one was seated near them, so more than once, Riley used the popcorn bucket to hide his hand sliding high on Brandon's thigh, brushing against his crotch. He didn't try to push his luck since neither of them wanted to cause a disturbance, but they traded furtive glances full of promise.

"I never realized how many episodes there were," Riley said when they finally headed back outside a few hours later.

"Watching all of them takes about fifteen hours." Brandon fell into step beside him. "I looked it up. And the ticket is good for three days, so we can come back for more."

"I remember catching the reruns on cable now and then. I never realized how many of the jokes were for grownups."

"Yeah, my mom always laughed louder than I did, and then she'd say—'you'll understand when you grow up,'" Brandon replied. "And she was right."

Riley liked that the conversation flowed naturally, and they didn't have trouble finding things to talk about. He thought about Brandon's confession about not being able to read his thoughts and found it didn't bother him. *I'd rather talk about what I'm thinking or feeling than just "think" at each other anyhow.*

All they lacked was privacy to follow up on their racy conversation from the night before. Riley understood that in a small town where everyone knew everyone else, making out in the men's room was a bad idea. In good weather, they might have been able to find a secluded spot outside, but Riley didn't fancy freezing his bits off when he had definite ideas of how to put them to use in the near future.

Going back to his motel was a possibility, but he wasn't quite ready to explain his security precautions. *Not yet. I don't want to admit that I come with complications.*

"Next time, I'll cook," Brandon offered as if he really could read Riley's thoughts—or maybe something in his body language gave him away. "My cabin isn't far, and we could watch a movie or play video games…or something…afterward."

Riley gave his mittened hand a squeeze. "I vote for 'or something.'"

Brandon grinned. "I was hoping you'd say that. I'm not a gourmet cook, but I can put a decent meal on the table."

"I don't need anything fancy," Riley replied. "I'm all about the company."

Brandon paused and turned toward him, bending down to sweep a kiss across his lips. "I like the sound of that. Maybe next time, you can spend the night so we don't have to worry about getting you home safely."

"I think that sounds like a plan."

Reluctantly, they said goodbye at Riley's SUV. He had an early appointment with Dr. Jeffries the next day, and although Riley would have gladly foregone a few hours' sleep for living out some of his fantasies with Brandon, the town was closing up for the night.

"Drive safely." Brandon nuzzled Riley's ear as he dropped his voice. "See you for lunch tomorrow."

Riley kissed him, reaching up to run his hand over the back of

Brandon's head and toying with the fringe of dark hair that peeked out beneath his hat. "Sleep tight."

Riley sat in the SUV for a moment and reviewed the last few hours of security camera clips, relieved that no one except housekeeping had been near his room. Anxiety and a fear of heartbreak came with being a Gemini, and Riley freely admitted he had both.

When he walked into the room, he saw the message light blinking on the phone and frowned, wondering what was wrong. He dialed the office, expecting to get a night clerk.

"Do you have a minute?" Steve, the motel manager, answered. "I need to talk to you about something."

"Sure," Riley replied, feeling his good mood dissipate. "I'm in the room now."

"Be right over."

A few minutes later, Riley let Steve into the room. "What's up?"

Steve held up his phone, showing photos of the security cameras Riley had placed outside his room trained on the door. "Want to explain? Before I involve the sheriff?"

Riley sighed and sat down on the end of the bed. "I have a stalker ex-boyfriend. I filed a restraining order with the sheriff as soon as I came to town. Hopefully, he won't find out where I am or bother to drive this far if he does. But I'm afraid of him, and I wanted to be able to tell if anyone had been messing with the locks."

Steve was quiet for a moment. "Show me where all the cameras are."

Riley pointed out the small devices, wondering if he'd be packing his things and going back to the larger hotel.

"Nothing concealed or recording any other rooms?" Steve asked.

Riley shook his head. "No, you can clearly see them. On the peephole and on my room's door and window. He noted the door alarm and other precautions. "I'm not making a sex tape, and I'm not trying to infringe on anyone's privacy. I came to Fox Hollow to make a fresh start, and I'm scared my ex will try to interfere."

Steve ran a hand over his face as if deliberating what to say next. "I'm going to talk to the sheriff and our lawyer. I understand your situation, and I want you to be safe. I also have to protect the privacy of our other guests. Someone else might not have the same motives installing portable cameras, and it could get ugly."

"Do you want me to leave?"

Steve shook his head. "No. Sit tight—it's already late. I'll talk to the sheriff in the morning. We'll figure something out. I'm sorry that you have to worry about something like that."

"Thanks."

When Steve left, Riley fell back on the bed staring at the ceiling as his thoughts swirled.

I've got no reason to think Tate would look for me here. Or to think that he'd bother with the long drive, even if he found me. But I can't stop looking over my shoulder.

THE NEXT MORNING, Riley left the cameras in place when he went to his appointment with Dr. Jeffries at the Fox Institute. One of the things he already liked about the Institute was the collegial atmosphere and how well people seemed to get along. He didn't need to be psychic to pick up on good vibes and the absence of a tense undercurrent that was so often a part of other workplaces.

"You look like you've got a lot on your mind." Jeffries joined Riley in the conference room before the session started.

Riley debated how much to say, but since they were going to be spending the morning exploring the bounds of his psychic immunity, he figured he needed to explain what had happened at the hotel and his worries. Jeffries listened without interrupting and wore a concerned expression.

"Thank you for trusting me with your story," Jeffries replied. "I'm sorry that you've had to deal with that situation, although I know it's more common than people like to believe. I'd like to help any way I can. First, because you deserve to be safe. And second, if you're stressed and feel unsafe, the research project isn't going to be accurate."

"What did you have in mind?" Riley's heart soared when he realized the professor was willing to be an ally.

"I understand Steve's concerns, but liability cuts both ways. If you were to misuse the cameras to spy on other guests, laws exist to deal with that. Given your situation with your ex, precautions seem to me to be in order."

"Thank you." Riley felt relieved that the professor understood.

"For what it's worth, I can put in a good worth with Steve and the sheriff. If you can't work something out with the motel, I can see about getting you a room in our dorms. I arranged the motel for you because it gives you more privacy and an efficiency apartment. The dorms are just that—dorms. But it's an option. Don't worry—we'll find something that works."

Riley appreciated Jeffries's support and that he understood the risk. That went a long way toward easing Riley's worry, and while it didn't remove the threat, it did mean he wouldn't have to face it alone.

Today's session had Riley in the conference room meeting with psychics from the Institute, all with different abilities. Without being told in advance he was immune, they were supposed to try to figure out his gift, and the conversations would be recorded.

Riley felt oddly nervous as he waited for the first psychic. He had always considered being unreadable to be a deficiency, so having Jeffries regard it as a type of psychic ability made him reevaluate. *It would be nice to see it as a plus instead of a minus.*

His first visitor was a short, gray-haired woman named Cora, who reminded Riley a bit of his grandmother. She wore a sweater decorated with cheery snowmen over jeans and Timberlands.

"Well now, you're a puzzle," Cora said once they were seated. She raised her chin as if to see him better and focused intently. "What's going on with you, hmm?" After studying him intently, her eyes narrowed.

"You're conscious, so I should be able to pick up something from your thoughts, but I can't. Pick a word and think it over and over."

The first one to pop into Riley's thoughts was "moose" and the image of the elegant buck he had spotted outside the hotel. He closed his eyes and silently repeated the word as he kept the image in mind.

"Odd. Your body language says you're relaxed and cooperative, but you're not 'transmitting.' There's a peaceful blank where your thoughts should be," Cora added. "I will say that you're a nice change from most people—their thoughts are a loud, jumbled mess most of the time. It's…calming."

Over the next two hours, Riley met ten different psychics with varied abilities. Some were telepaths, while others read auras, told fortunes, or used casual touch to make a mental contact. They all were surprised at how closed off Riley was to them—and how little their gifts could tell them about him.

"I'm good at body language, and I can pick up some clues from that, but I'm not hearing or seeing anything from your mind," a seer named Jim told Riley. "I've never met anyone like you."

Brandon said he could pick up emotions even if he couldn't read my thoughts. Do we have some kind of special link? He remembered Brandon saying "mate" in his dream. *I thought that was only a shifter thing. Isn't it?*

Jeffries came to join him for a lunch of cold Italian sub sandwiches, kettle chips, and chocolate chip cookies. For having spent the morning being stared at without doing much else, Riley was surprised at how hungry he was.

"I've gotten reports back from the psychics," Jeffries said in between chips. "Now I want to hear your side of things."

Riley considered for a moment and sipped his Coke. "Other than feeling like the main attraction in a sideshow? Come see the curious case of the Silent Man," he joked.

"I'm sorry if we made you feel like that," Jeffries apologized.

Riley made a dismissive gesture. "It's not like you sold tickets. They were all very polite—and extremely interested. Some of them tried so hard to connect I thought smoke might come out of their ears. But mostly, I just got stared at a lot by rather frustrated people who couldn't figure out how I fritzed their radar."

Jeffries laughed. "I wouldn't have said it that way, but you're absolutely right. You're quite the mystery, and I suspect you'll be the talk of the Institute until someone comes up with a theory."

"Gotta be famous for something, I guess." Riley took a bite of his pickle spear.

"Other than being stared at, did you notice any other feelings or sensations?"

Riley thought for a moment, replaying his memories. "Not like when I'm with Brandon."

Jeffries raised an eyebrow. "Oh? What's different?"

Riley felt his cheeks color. *Besides the fact that I'm gone for him?* "Brandon told me he's telepathic, but he can only get a surface read of my emotions. None of the people I met with here mentioned that."

"Interesting."

Riley took a deep breath for courage. "Do you believe in fated mates?"

Jeffries gave him an evaluating look. "Tell me what that term means to you, and I'll give you an answer."

Riley balled up his empty sandwich wrapper and stuffed it into the chip bag. "You've said Fox Hollow is a haven for psychics—and shifters. I know psychics are real, so I'm going to have to assume shifters are too. Maybe it's just in romance books, but 'fated mates' or soulmates are two people who are somehow destined to be together—sometimes in more than one lifetime. It makes for a great story, but is it real?"

Jeffries paused for a moment to finish his bite of sandwich before replying. "Yes."

"Really? Do both people have to be a shifter for it to work?" Riley hadn't expected how his heart soared at the possibility.

"No, although it might be more common—or at least more widely recognized—in the shifter community," Jeffries answered, and Riley had the feeling the man was choosing his words carefully.

"Brandon and I have been seeing each other since I came to town," Riley said. "It's going well, I think. He's a great guy, and I feel safe with him. He told me about his telepathy, and that's when it came up that he could still pick up on my emotions, and…I know this is going to sound crazy, but I had this dream where he said we were mates."

"Have you ever had any reason to think someone else close to you with an emotional attachment has been able to read anything from you?" Jeffries looked intrigued but seemed to ignore his comment about mates.

Riley thought back over his past relationships. Some fizzled, others went down in flames, and then there was Tate.

"I'm pretty sure my stalker ex is a psi-vamp."

That got Jeffries's attention. "Can you explain why?"

"Tate was an emotional rollercoaster. The highs were high, and the lows were awful. We either were head-over-heels or fighting. I noticed that even during the good times I always felt more tired than usual, worn out," Riley said. "Then I realized that Tate was orchestrating the situation, either love bombing or starting nasty fights. I was fading, and he seemed to be having a grand time. So I broke it off, and then I ran away. To here."

Jeffries drummed his fingers on the table. "That makes sense because a psi-vamp works differently from most psychics. He wasn't reading your thoughts; he was tapping into your energy. Emotions give 'flavor' to energy, especially extremes like joy or anger. It didn't matter that you're a psychic immune—that wasn't the source of his 'food.'"

Riley couldn't resist a shudder. Now that he was out and away from Tate, he remembered how he sometimes felt not just worn down but consumed. *I didn't realize it was literal.*

"Have you ever had something odd happen with anyone else where there's been a strong emotional bond?"

"I'll have to think about it, but not off the top of my head," Riley answered.

Riley knew Jeffries was trying to help him, but he also recognized that his situation clearly intrigued the man on an academic level. *If there are other immunes like me—and there must be—maybe he can find out something that helps them too.*

"Being immune might have been what made it possible for you to get away from him," Jeffries said. "He could feed off your emotions, but he couldn't use your deepest thoughts against you."

Riley hated the idea that his situation with Tate could have been worse. *It was bad enough. I felt like I barely saved my skin.*

He struggled to come up with the right way to word his next question. "How do I know if someone's a shifter?"

"Unless you see them shifting or they tell you, you don't." Jeffries sank his balled-up wrapper in the trash can in a neat dunk. "Around here, it's safest to assume people are unless told differently. In case you wondered—I'm not."

"I'm guessing that 'outing' people as shifters is impolite."

"Very. If they want you to know, they'll tell you. Not everyone in Fox Hollow is a shifter, but nearly everyone has some sort of magic or ability. The few who don't are family to someone who does."

Is Brandon a shifter? Are the books right, and shifters recognize their mate when they meet? But if he believes we might be mates, why hasn't he told me? He trusted me enough to tell me he's a telepath.

Then again, since he can't read me, maybe he isn't sure enough of how I feel about him yet. We haven't been seeing each other long.

"What's it like, knowing which of the people around you can become something else?"

Jeffries smiled. "A bit like living in an enchanted forest, at least that's how I think of it. Once you know, you can pick up tidbits of their other side in their personality. Then it seems like hiding in plain sight."

Riley had promised to go to the comics store to meet a couple of Madden's friends for a role-playing game after he finished at the Institute. He thought about how Madden's twitchiness reminded him of a squirrel and how Sherri at the café made him think of a bear.

Maybe they really are.

"How does the shifter thing work? I'm not asking for secrets—I don't want to assume that what I've read in romance books is true."

"Definitely smart to challenge your sources." Jeffries chuckled. "Shifters can change at any time of the month, as opposed to weres, who can only change around the full moon. Shifters are born; weres are created, usually by a bite or the transfer of blood."

So werewolves are real too? I mean, why not?

Riley felt his world tilt a bit on its axis. *I already believe in psychics and psi-vamps. How much more of a stretch is it to believe in shifters and weres?*

"Some types of shifters can turn into any living creature, while others have a particular 'familiar' that is their changed shape," Jeffries said. "All of the shifters I'm aware of in Fox Hollow fall into the last category. They can change into one animal form, always the same.

Wolves, foxes, bears are what most people think of—but shifters can also be squirrels, otters, possums, or raccoons, for example. Wild animals, usually, although we do have a couple of goat shifters."

How cool is that? If Brandon really is a shifter, I wonder what he is? Something big, probably. A deer? Do they have reindeer around here? Elk? Maybe a moose.

As soon as he thought the word "moose" something settled in his mind, validating the choice.

I've got a major crush on a moose. Moose shifter. He thought about the festival he and Brandon had just attended and the Bullwinkle movies. *I just went to a moose festival with a guy who can turn into a moose. That's entirely too meta. No wonder he was laughing at the jokes.*

When was he going to tell me? What do I have to do to earn his trust?

Jeffries cleared his throat. "I don't have to read your mind to figure out the drift of what you're thinking. People in these parts generally reveal their shifter side once they know and trust you well enough to keep their secret. That's a big reason why we're so careful about who can live here year-round. There's a lot of hiding in plain sight that goes on, but for the most part, folks here are proud of who and what they are and don't like to hide it."

"That's a lot to think about," Riley admitted. "Thanks for trusting me."

Jeffries smiled. "We have a lot of folks who talk about fate and destiny. I don't think it's a coincidence when people are drawn to Fox Hollow. They often find out it's where they're meant to be."

———

SINCE HE HAD FINISHED the research for the day at the Institute, Riley headed to the comics shop. He was a little early, but that gave him time to browse. *Maybe picking up some new manga will take my mind off Tate. Or maybe Madden can get me hooked on a comics series.*

When he arrived, Madden was talking with two men Riley hadn't seen before, a taller, muscular man with dark hair and brown eyes and a more slightly built blond with bright blue eyes.

"Hi, Riley! I'd like you to meet Mico," he indicated the taller of the two men, "and Jack. By the way—Jack is responsible for those awesome donuts at the café."

"I'm already your devoted fan," Riley said. "Your donuts are amazing."

"Mico and Jack are regulars here," Madden told Riley. "We play RPGs once a week—it would be great if you could join us." The two men enthusiastically agreed. "In fact, we're just about to start a game. Want to join us? It'll take about an hour."

"Sure." Riley was pleased to be asked. He got a good feeling from Mico and Jack. Puzzles, games, and good conversations were so Gemini. After having to give up things he liked to keep peace with Tate, Riley loved embracing his real interests again.

"Riley's new in town—he's going to be playing his guitar at the hotel a couple of nights a week," Madden told the others.

"That's you? I've seen posters. Cool. We both work nights, but we'd love to see you play when we have the chance," Jack said, and Mico nodded in agreement.

After his conversation with Jeffries, Riley felt certain that Madden was a squirrel shifter. Mico's shadowed eyes made Riley think of a raccoon. And Jack's pale skin and hair and long fingers made him wonder—*possum?*

Jeffries said it was like living in an enchanted forest. I feel like I've walked into a fairy tale. He felt wonder and a surge of gratitude at finding such a special place. *I think I want to stay here. Could Brandon be the one for me?*

Madden set up the gaming table in the back. His boyfriend Elias came out to run the register while Madden and the others gamed. Jack put out a box of donuts and a large container of coffee from the café.

"Fuel for the journey," he told them with a grin.

Mico explained the rules to the adventure game while Madden dealt cards and arranged the playing pieces. Riley had always been intrigued by RPGs but had never been able to interest Tate in playing. Now, he had the chance to indulge his interests and make new friends.

Madden ran the game, combining strategy, humor, and whimsy. The three of them had clearly spent a lot of time together and had an easy rapport, but they made an effort to include Riley and make sure he was part of the conversation.

Halfway through, Riley felt himself relax. No one seemed to care much about winning beyond some friendly competition. The others traded good-natured jibes without malice. He realized this was the most relaxed he had felt, other than when he was with Brandon, in a very long time.

The game ended too soon, and Riley was surprised that the hour moved so quickly. "That was a lot of fun. I'd love to play again soon."

"We can arrange that." Madden grinned. Mico and Jack, clearly a couple, said goodbye, and Riley lingered to help Madden put things away.

"Something on your mind?" Madden asked as he closed up the box and put it on a shelf behind the counter.

"That was a lot of fun. Your friends are great," Riley said, feeling wistful.

"I'm sure they can become your friends too," Madden replied. "They're both pretty chill. The only difficulty is finding times to get together since they work nights. Mico drives a garbage truck, and Jack does his baking on the night shift. By the way—Mico's also an artist. Found objects. He does some really cool stuff."

"I like that sort of thing." Riley loved quirky things and offbeat art, another point of contention with Tate.

I'm done with Tate. What he thought doesn't matter anymore.

"So where are you headed now?" Madden bustled around, putting items back where they belonged and straightening displays.

"I'm supposed to meet Brandon and go for a short hike, then get dinner," Riley said. Something in his tone must have caught Madden's attention since the other man turned to look at him.

"Brandon, huh? He's a good guy."

"We seem to hit it off," Riley confessed. "I'm looking forward to seeing him again."

Madden turned to look at him and tilted his head. In Riley's mind, he could almost imagine a squirrel tail flicking behind him. "Have you thought more about whether you're staying in Fox Hollow?" His tone took on a protective edge.

"I'm considering that. I really like it here."

"Whatever you decide, make sure you're clear to Brandon so you're both on the same page," Madden warned.

He's worried about Brandon getting hurt if I don't stay. I've fallen for him. Does that mean Brandon is falling for me too?

He sighed. "I had a bad breakup a while ago. So I'm a little gun-shy. But I like Brandon enough to get past it. I just hope he feels the same way."

"Brandon doesn't always say what he's thinking or feeling right away," Madden said. "Be patient, and if there's a spark, it'll happen. As for you being skittish—Brandon's a real catch for someone who knows how to treat him right."

"I would never do anything to hurt Brandon," Riley said. "He's a big part of what I like here."

"As long as we're clear." Warning delivered, Madden brightened. "Go have fun on your hike. And come back whenever you can—I'll have some new manga in on Thursday."

RILEY MULLED Madden's comments as he drove to the trailhead where he was supposed to meet Brandon. He brightened when he saw Brandon's Suburban. Brandon was leaning against it, toying with his phone.

Riley admired Brandon's long legs and broad shoulders, and the careless mop of brown hair that always seemed to fall into his eyes. *Yep, I'm properly smitten.*

"How's your day been?" Brandon greeted him and gave Riley the once-over. Riley hoped Brandon liked what he saw.

"Busy. I can tell you while we walk. And Madden says hello."

Brandon glanced at him. "Oh, yeah?"

Riley filled him in about the game with Mico and Jack, but he left out the details of his conversation with Madden. From the slight blush that crept into the tips of Brandon's ears, he wondered if Brandon had also confided in Madden about him.

"I'm glad you found the store. Those are all good guys, and it's a great hangout. Come on—we don't want to lose the light. It's a short hike, but we want to see where we're going."

Brandon led the way, and Riley followed behind, enjoying the view of his guide's firm ass and muscular legs as much as the forest surrounding them. Brandon kept up a constant patter, and Riley figured he was going into "guide mode." He listened as Brandon talked about the forest and the types of trees, the way the nearby lakes formed the streams and tributaries.

"Welcome to Buttermilk Falls." Brandon stepped aside so Riley got the full view.

A torrent of water tumbled over rocks, churning up white froth that earned the name. Snow clung to the edges, but the roiling water remained ice-free. It wasn't Niagara, but it was still a nice payoff for a short, easy hike. Riley took in a deep breath of balsam and felt the cold spray on his face.

"Very nice. The forest is beautiful. Thank you for bringing me here."

"You did great on the hike—and it gets easier with practice," Brandon told him.

Riley's Gemini soul warmed at the compliment. This was exactly the kind of quality time he treasured with a partner—something Tate had never given him.

"Thanks. It wasn't as hard as I thought it would be," Riley replied. "You're a good guide. I'd follow you anywhere," he added with a wink.

"There are plenty of short hikes like this if you want to see more." Brandon grinned at the obvious flirtation. "I'd be happy to show you."

"I'm really falling in love with Fox Hollow," Riley admitted. *And I'm pretty sure I've already fallen in love with you.*

"Next time, I'll take you cross-country skiing. We can practice in my yard so you can get the hang of it without committing to a long trail. When the snow is deep, it's actually easier than trying to walk."

"I'm game," Riley said. "Sounds like a plan. Speaking of snow— what happened to the big storm we were supposed to get?"

"We got a reprieve but not a pass. Apparently, it slowed down, but that just means it'll be stronger when it gets here. We're still on its path," Brandon replied.

"We've still got time for dinner before your gig," Brandon checked the time. "And then if you want—and you're not too tired—we can go back to my place and chill."

Riley reached for his hand and gave it a squeeze. "I'd like that a lot."

They ate at the bar at the hotel since the afternoon had slipped away fast. Riley loved how comfortable he felt talking about everything and nothing with Brandon. He didn't need to impress or entertain—just recounting the day seemed to interest Brandon, who was a good listener.

Riley's phone alarm pinged. He leaned in and gave Brandon a quick kiss. "Gotta get ready. Can you stay?"

Brandon nodded. "Absolutely. Can you come home with me tonight?"

The promise in that question sent heat racing through Riley's blood. "Absolutely."

A slow, broad smile lit Brandon's face. "Looking forward to it."

Half an hour later, Riley walked up to the stage with his guitar, pleased that more seats were filled than the night before. Brandon kept his spot at the bar and gave Riley an encouraging nod. Riley didn't know the rest of the people when he sat down to play, but as his first set continued, he saw Dr. Jeffries slip into the room, followed by Madden and Elias.

Despite how busy the day had been, Riley's mood soared, and he channeled his feelings into his voice. He made sure to glance around the room as he sang, acknowledging the audience, but his gaze always returned to Brandon.

Before he went out that morning, Riley had sketched out set notes over breakfast. He made sure he knew the words and had the lyrics on his phone, which had a holder on the mic stand. They were classics, ranging across decades, but guaranteed crowd-pleasers.

Once again, the audience rose to the occasion, clapping along, joining him on the chorus, or enthusiastically doing a call and response. Even having had a busy day, Riley felt his energy rise from their interaction and reflected his joy into his songs.

"Great set," Brandon praised when Riley retreated to the bar for his break. Brandon handed him a ginger ale. "Figured you'd want something to drink."

Riley accepted the glass with a nod of thanks. "Did you like the songs?"

"They're a great match for your voice. The crowd was definitely with you. I'm impressed. You're really good."

Riley felt his cheeks heat with the praise. "Glad you liked it. There are a few more people in the audience tonight than before—maybe word is getting around."

Dr. Jeffries wandered toward them. "Nice job, Riley. I had to stop by and see for myself. I think you'll do well here."

Madden and Elias joined them. "Loved the song choices," Madden enthused with his usual energy. "You picked a bunch of my favorites."

Brandon slipped an arm around Riley. "I think he's a good fit." He added a squeeze for emphasis.

They chatted for a few minutes while Riley sipped his drink, but his phone chime reminded him to return to the stage.

"Knock 'em dead," Brandon told him and gave Riley a kiss on the cheek. If Madden or Elias were surprised, neither showed it.

Several more people drifted in during Riley's second set, filling the bar, if not all the tables. They smiled and tapped their fingers and toes to the music, swaying with the beat. Riley might not be able to read their minds, but their body language gave him plenty of feedback, and their enjoyment fed him energy.

When he finished his second set, he stood and took a bow to the applause. Brandon was waiting for him after Riley packed up his guitar and got his coat.

"Are you too tired—"

"Are you kidding? After I play, I'm positively buzzed from the crowd's energy," Riley interrupted.

Brandon grinned. "That's what I was hoping you'd say."

They left Riley's Pilot in the hotel lot. Riley piled into Brandon's

Suburban with his guitars and a small backpack he had brought from the motel that morning, just in case their plans worked out.

"I'll warn you—my cabin isn't fancy, but it's snug in the winter and has a great view in the summer," Brandon said as they headed out of town.

"Did you build it?"

"Not from scratch. A lot of cabins around these parts were built in the first half of the last century, before the War," Brandon replied. "They built things to last. I got a good deal when the previous owner decided he'd had enough of winter and wanted to move south. I made some adjustments because it wasn't built for someone my size, but the bones of the place were solid."

The "cabin" was more of a cross between a bungalow and a chalet, made of logs with a large stone chimney.

"That looks solid—and warm," Riley said as they climbed out of the SUV.

"Warm enough that if I've got a good fire going, I have to crack the windows even in the winter because it gets very toasty." Brandon angled ahead of Riley so he could open the door.

Riley stepped inside and looked around as Brandon turned on the lights.

"Wow, this is beautiful." Riley looked around. The walls were a combination of logs and tongue-and-groove knotty pine. A large stone fireplace dominated one end of the living room. The wood slat ceiling was open to the beams but not vaulted to conserve heat. Riley thought the overstuffed furnishings looked homey and comfortable.

"It's not trendy," Brandon said. "But it's warm and comfortable in the winter, and the windows have good cross-breezes in the summer."

Bookshelves lined the wall on either side of the massive fireplace, filled with hardcovers, paperbacks, and a few knickknacks. Framed landscape paintings hung on the side walls. Riley had already learned to recognize them as the Hudson River School style.

And absolutely no antlers or taxidermied deer heads.

Because if Brandon is a moose shifter, that would be like me hanging a skull on the wall. Ew.

"I have chili in the slow cooker—hope that's okay," Brandon said as

Riley followed him into the kitchen, which had clearly been updated from its original form with modern appliances and butcher-block counters. The aroma of the chili filled the cabin, and Riley's stomach rumbled.

"It smells great. How can I help?"

"The garlic bread is frozen, so it just pops into the oven once that's pre-heated, and I'm going to make a salad. How about just keeping me company?"

"I can handle that."

Riley settled in at the farmhouse-style table and watched as Brandon moved around the kitchen like a pro.

"How did you learn to cook?" Riley asked.

"I got tired of eating crappy food. Seriously—I was tired of takeout, microwaved meals, and frozen dinners and decided it couldn't be that hard to figure out some basic meals. And I was right."

Brandon handed him spoons and napkins to set the table, then put bowls and glasses on the counter.

"I've got water, milk, and beer. Since you're staying the night and neither of us have to drive, I'd say go for the beer," Brandon suggested.

"Sounds like a plan."

Once the garlic bread was ready, Brandon set out toppings and bowls. "Help yourself. If you want something you don't see, just ask."

Conversation stayed light over dinner, talking about favorite television shows and upcoming movies. Afterward, Riley cleared the table while Brandon put leftovers away and loaded the dishwasher.

This feels so comfortable. So…normal. I could get really used to it.

They debated which movie to watch and finally agreed on an action flick they had both seen before, then settled on the couch together. Despite the size of the sofa, they sat so their legs touched from hip to knee, and Brandon put his arm around Riley's shoulders.

That was a little different since Riley was used to being the larger partner, but he leaned into Brandon's side and decided he liked it.

Not long into the movie, Brandon shifted to face him and met his gaze as he leaned forward to kiss him. Riley turned for a better angle and slipped his hand up along Brandon's face. He let his tongue flick along Brandon's lower lip, and Brandon opened to him, deepening the kiss.

Brandon's hands cupped Riley's shoulders, then slid down his arms. One hand splayed on Riley's chest and slowly rubbed circles around his hard nipples.

"This okay?" Brandon murmured. He leaned forward to nuzzle Riley's neck, mouthing his way from ear to collarbone.

"Very okay." Riley was already breathless. He let his hands roam, combing through Brandon's soft brown hair, tracing the line of his jaw, then lower to the firm pecs. "Just so you know—I test regularly, and I'm negative."

"Me too."

For a while, they just made out, kissing and touching, the movie forgotten. Riley got brave and climbed onto Brandon's lap, knees straddling his thighs.

"Still okay?" he murmured.

Brandon gripped his ass and gave his cheeks a squeeze. "Oh, yeah."

Riley could feel Brandon's cock through his jeans, hard and size-able. He ground down, achingly erect, and Brandon thrust up to meet him. At this rate, kissing, touching, and rubbing was going to make everything over too soon.

"Can I blow you?" Riley drew back from a kiss. Brandon's lust-blown dark eyes met his, eager and hungry.

"Definitely."

Riley slid down between Brandon's knees. Brandon spread his legs and leaned back, giving him access. Riley kept eye contact the whole time as he worked Brandon's belt free, teased the zipper open slowly, and pushed the jeans down to give him full access to his boxer briefs and the prominent package inside.

"Mmmm." Riley leaned in, mouthing along the bulge in Brandon's briefs, taking in his scent, pleased that there was already a wet spot.

"Not going to last real long this time," Brandon panted. He tangled his fingers in Riley's hair, stroking, not pushing. His other arm was spread out along the back of the couch, hand clenching the pillow. "It's been a while."

Riley hummed a response and felt Brandon jolt as if stung. *Sensitive.* He pushed the briefs down and licked Brandon's long, thick cock from root to head, then began to swirl his tongue over the knob and through the slit. One hand gripped the base since Riley wasn't sure he could deep throat that much without practice, while the other reached lower to fondle Brandon's balls.

"So good," Brandon moaned.

Riley kept a steady rhythm, even though his own cock ached for relief. He coated one finger in spit and slid back to rim Brandon's hole. Brandon cried out, bucked forward, and spilled down Riley's throat.

Riley swallowed as much as he could, losing rivulets down both sides of his mouth. He pulled off with a *pop* and then licked up what had spilled.

Brandon drew him up and kissed him, tasting himself on Riley's lips.

"Your turn." Brandon unfastened Riley's belt and pulled him to stand between Brandon's knees. That made it easy to peel his jeans and underwear down to his thighs, letting his rock-hard cock spring free.

Brandon pushed his face into Riley's groin and breathed in his scent. His large hands gripped Riley's ass hard enough Riley thought he might see fingerprints and welcomed the reminder. Brandon lightly kissed and nipped his way along Riley's thighs before returning his attention to Riley's weeping cock.

He murmured something Riley didn't quite catch, either "mine" or "mate," before getting to work. His tongue traced the veins and ran up and down the shaft before Brandon closed his lips around the head and began to suck while still keeping his tongue in play.

Riley groaned. "Yes. Like that." He hadn't been with anyone since his breakup, and nothing compared to the real thing.

Brandon set a mind-blowing pace as he slipped two fingers behind Riley's cock and searched for the perfect spot on his taint—*right there*—that would stroke his prostate deep inside.

Riley came hard, feeling his orgasm rise from his core and sweep over him in a rush. For a few seconds, he thought he had whited out, knees like jelly as if he would collapse if Brandon's hands let go of his ass.

His intense climax made it hard to think, but as the buzz cleared, Riley realized that more than ever before, he felt an intense connection to Brandon through the act, different from what he had experienced with any other partner. *Fated mates?*

Brandon reached for tissues from a box on the end table to clean them both up and tucked Riley away, doing up his pants. He shifted to lie longwise and pulled Riley back onto the couch with him between his legs.

"Good enough?" Brandon asked, his voice a little deeper than usual.

"Definitely," Riley breathed, still feeling blissed out.

Brandon wrapped his arms around Riley. "I'm glad you're here."

Riley let his head fall back against Brandon's solid chest. "I'm glad we're here together."

I'm over the moon for him. Does he feel the same for me?

Then again, if we're really fated mates, it's supposed to go both ways, right?

They sat intertwined through the end of the movie, with Riley protected within the embrace of Brandon's arms and thighs. He was surprised how much of a turn-on it was to be the "little spoon" and smiled, just letting go and enjoying the sensation. Brandon pressed a kiss to the junction of Riley's neck and shoulder, and added a light nip, then sucked a hickey for good measure.

Mating bite? Marking me? Somehow that's sexy as hell, he thought, remembering some of the stories he'd read.

"Unless you want to fall asleep like this—which would be bad for our necks—we should close up and move to the bed. I promise you it's more comfortable," Brandon said in a low rumble next to Riley's ear.

Riley didn't bounce back for round two as quickly as in his teens but damned if that voice didn't make his spent cock manage to twitch. *There's always the morning.*

"Comfortable." Riley wiggled his hips against Brandon's groin.

"Save that thought for tomorrow," Brandon chuckled. "Come on. I'll even let you have first crack at the bathroom."

Reluctantly, Riley sighed and stood up, immediately noting the loss of warmth and security from Brandon's embrace. He helped Brandon close up and allowed himself to be led to the back corridor.

"Two bedrooms and a bathroom in between, and a linen closet for good measure," Brandon noted about the floor plan. He opened a door and brought Riley into the master bedroom.

"I made the bed just for you," Brandon teased.

The room looked as comfortable and homey as the rest of the cabin. A few framed personal photos sat on the nightstand, which held a Craftsman-style lamp. More bookshelves were filled with books and DVDs, as well as small items—including a little statue of a moose.

"Do you need a toothbrush? I just went to the dentist last week and have a new one still in the 'goody bag,'" Brandon offered.

"Actually remembered to bring my own." Riley hefted his backpack. He had grabbed essential toiletries, fresh underwear, and a new shirt and socks, plus sleep pants and a long-sleeved T-shirt. He didn't mention how obsessively he had thought about preparing for their date night, going over and over his packing list.

"I'll lock up while you get ready," Brandon said. "Go ahead and get comfy. The right side of the bed is yours."

The bathroom had clearly been updated with a walk-in shower and a soaking tub big enough to accommodate Brandon—and maybe a partner. Riley washed and changed, taking pride in his still reddened and puffy lips like a memento.

I'm already in deep. I sure hope Brandon feels the same way. Recalling the intensity in Brandon's gaze and the gentle possessiveness in his touch, Riley thought the chances were good that his affection was returned.

Riley finished and took his backpack with him to the bedroom, where he crawled under the covers. The flannel sheets were comfortably worn and soft, and the bedding smelled of balsam, citrus, and something unmistakably *Brandon.*

He had just gotten comfortable when Brandon came in from the hallway, shirtless in sleep pants covered with a moose pattern. Riley took the chance to get a good look at Brandon's muscular arms and impressive chest. A dark thatch of hair covered Brandon's pecs with a happy trail that led down below the drawstring of his pants.

"Aren't you going to be cold?" Riley shivered in sympathy. Despite the cabin's snug design, it was still winter, as the sound of the wind outside reminded him. Riley was comfortable beneath the covers in his pajamas but decided being naked would need friction and activity to keep him warm.

"I run hot." Brandon shrugged. "Are you comfortable?"

"I'm sure I'll be perfectly warm once you're here." Riley patted the other side of the bed. He looked forward to falling asleep with his head on Brandon's shoulder and an arm across his belly. Brandon nuzzled his face against the top of Riley's head.

"You smell so good," Brandon murmured.

"Must be my shampoo," Riley joked, sleepy and fucked out.

"Nah. It's all you. Maple and anise. Best scents in the world."

Maple and anise? That's what I smell like to him? I wonder if it's a moose thing.

Riley sniffed the air, getting a balsam scent and a musky undertone that was all Brandon. He felt safe, protected, and cherished.

It might be too early to fall in love, but I'm definitely headed that direction. I could get used to the idea of having a mate.

Riley knew he couldn't stay tangled up with Brandon all night without combusting from the other man's body heat, but he resolved to stay close as long as he could.

I haven't been in Fox Hollow long, and I'm already sure I want to stay forever. I've got to figure out a plan. I can't count on my music alone to support me. Maybe Madden and his friends will have some ideas. I've got to stand by my moose.

7

BRANDON

BRANDON WOKE HOT AND HORNY. HE BLAMED BOTH ON THE EXTREMELY attractive man sleeping on the other side of his bed—his mate and now his lover.

Riley's amazing scent had grown stronger since they brought each other to climax, and Brandon knew that would continue until they consummated their relationship, and he placed a mating bite.

His cock was painfully hard, tenting his sleep pants. Brandon pressed his hand against the base, trying to reduce the urgency. If they were an established couple, Brandon would have awakened Riley with a sleepy hand job or picked up the blow job where he had left off.

But they had a lot of territory to cover before they reached that point of comfort and consent and a lot of communicating, so he sighed as he willed his errant cock to soften with thoughts of shredded wheat and cleaning out the refrigerator.

When that didn't work, Brandon kissed Riley lightly on the shoulder and slipped out of bed, padding to the bathroom to take care of his "problem." He thought about taking a run in his fur, but the likelihood of discovery was too high, and they hadn't yet had the "talk."

Dreading that conversation was the dick-wilter Brandon had been searching for, deflating the earlier urgency.

How do I tell him? "You know how some people have hidden talents? I can turn into a moose."

Too direct.

Did you ever daydream about being able to be your favorite animal? I've got something cool to show you.

Ugh.

Hey Riley—watch me turn a person into a moose. This time, he thought the words in Bullwinkle's voice.

Definitely not.

Say it with pride. Claim your heritage, his moose spoke up.

It's complicated.

Reaching twigs at the top of a tree is complicated, his inner moose said with a snort. *It's not difficult—just tell him the truth.*

What if it scares him off? He's new to Fox Hollow. All this stuff isn't what he's used to, Brandon fretted.

If he's really our fated mate, he'll understand.

Brandon wished he could have his moose's confidence. Yes, Riley had been chill about psychics and learning more about his own gift. And he had certainly heard by now that Fox Hollow was also a haven for shifters. But Brandon feared that there might be too big a gap for Riley between considering that shifters might exist and learning that the guy he had gone to bed with could turn into a moose.

You won't know until you try.

Brandon went to the kitchen and started a fresh pot of coffee, found a box of pancake mix, and put bacon in the oven. While his moose was vegetarian, Brandon indulged in a few favorites—like bacon and hamburgers—in his human form.

Before long, Riley shuffled into the kitchen looking adorably rumpled. "Smells good." Riley made a beeline for the coffee maker.

"Mugs are up above, sugar is in the bowl on the counter," Brandon directed as he flipped the first batch of pancakes. "How did you sleep?"

"Really well. The bed was comfortable, and the company was even better." Riley gave him a broad wink as he filled his cup, and Brandon felt his heart jump.

"I hope you weren't too warm. I run hot," Brandon replied.

"Didn't bother me at all. Best sleep I've had in a while."

Brandon served up the first plate of pancakes and took the bacon out of the oven. He had already put a pitcher of maple syrup on the table. "Help yourself. I have to cook the rest of the pancakes. There's plenty of everything for both of us."

Riley dug in, and Brandon felt a deep sense of satisfaction to see him eat well.

We provide for our mate. His moose sounded pleased.

Brandon made a plate for himself and sat across from Riley. For several minutes, they focused on the food and coffee, and Brandon liked the comfortable domesticity. He had been content living alone without even considering a roommate. Now, he never wanted Riley to leave.

"Still want to learn a little about cross-country skiing this morning? I have an extra set of skis that shouldn't be too long for you," Brandon offered. "We don't even have to leave my yard—plenty of room to show you the basics. Then next time, we can try an easy trail."

Riley grinned. "Sure. Sounds fun. But if I'm hopeless at it, no fair laughing."

"I promise I won't laugh—cross my heart." Brandon made the motion over his chest.

When they finished the food and cleared the table, Riley came up behind Brandon and wrapped his arms around him. "Thanks for breakfast. And for last night."

Brandon turned, keeping Riley in his embrace, and kissed him. "My pleasure." They kissed for several minutes, and Brandon knew they were both growing hard.

"How about we shower together? It's big enough for two, and we can take care of each other before we get the day started." Brandon dropped to a low tone that made Riley shiver.

"That sounds like a great idea."

They walked toward the bathroom together. Brandon felt completely comfortable with Riley, despite the sexual tension that fairly crackled in the air around them.

"We can get dressed in the bedroom afterward. There's a little more elbow room. So don't worry about bringing in clothes—I've got plenty of towels."

Both men stripped and kicked their sleep pants toward the door. Brandon adjusted the water temperature. Riley made no bones about ogling Brandon.

"See something you like?" Brandon teased as he gave Riley a very thorough once-over.

"Oh, yeah."

Brandon stepped into the large shower and held out his hand for Riley. His gaze fell immediately to the purpled hickey on Riley's shoulder where a mating bite would go.

"I hope I didn't hurt you," he blurted.

Riley shook his head. "I like the reminder. It'll keep you with me when we're apart."

Brandon stepped under the warm water and drew Riley with him. They took turns washing each other's hair, although Brandon had to bend a bit for Riley to reach the top of his head. The shampoo smelled of mint and thyme, and the soap's cedar fragrance was earthy and grounding.

"Smells good," Riley said as Brandon carefully lathered and rinsed him. "And I like you touching me."

"Good thing, because I like touching you."

Brandon let his hand work its way down to Riley's cock, which rapidly hardened in his grip. "Let me take care of you," he murmured against Riley's neck, licking the tender hickey and getting a groan in response from his partner.

He kept one arm across Riley's chest to steady him and splayed his feet wide for support. Riley leaned back against him, letting his head fall on Brandon's shoulder. Brandon's hand, slick with conditioner, worked Riley's cock and stroked his balls. It didn't take long before Riley came all over Brandon's hand and splashed the far wall.

Brandon nipped gently at the hickey and Riley moaned. *Mate.*

With a contented sigh, Riley turned in Brandon's arms. "Come here," Riley growled.

Riley wasn't as tall as Brandon, but his solid, toned body supported Brandon as Riley began to stroke his cock. Riley peppered

Brandon's back with kisses and ground his still-soft cock against Brandon's ass.

"That's it," Riley coaxed as Brandon's breathing hitched. "Just enjoy it—and let go."

Moments later, Brandon cried out Riley's name as he shot, covering Riley's hand with his come.

"Good morning." Riley planted a kiss between Brandon's shoulders.

"You can wake me up like that any time," Brandon sighed.

They finished in the shower and toweled off. Both men skipped shaving and dressed quickly in the bedroom.

Brandon took Riley in his arms and drew him close. "I'm not rushing you or trying to make you feel pressured, but I want you in every way you'll have me. We can take our time. But I thought you ought to know."

"So many things I want to do with you." Riley shifted so their cocks brushed against each other. Even soft, the friction sent a jolt through Brandon.

"Good. We'll get to do all of them and then start over again," Brandon promised. "I want that too."

Tell him about me, his moose prodded. *We're a package deal.*

I will, Brandon promised. *When the time is right.*

His moose huffed in frustration and retreated to the back of Brandon's mind to sulk.

Brandon dried off Riley, taking his time to appreciate his partner's toned body, looking forward to learning everything that gave him pleasure. Riley returned the favor like a sensual ritual, and Brandon reveled in his nearness, and the intimacy in such a simple gesture.

Once they dressed, they got coats and boots and headed to Brandon's garage where the skis were stored.

"Once you get the hang of it, skiing is very peaceful," Brandon told him as he looked over the gear he had accumulated, including boots and skis in several sizes. "When you learn to move, it feels natural."

They found a set that fit Riley well enough to get him started and carried the gear outside.

"If you get hooked, you'll want to buy your own and have them properly fitted." Brandon helped Riley get into the boots and attach them to the skis. "But this is good enough to let you get started."

He made quick work of his own skis and saw Riley swaying, trying to keep his balance and afraid to move his feet.

"Here." Brandon laughed and handed Riley two poles. "Once you get used to the skis, you'll forget you've got them on. But at first, people say it's like having boards on their shoes."

"I'm afraid I'll fall over and not be able to get up," Riley admitted. "I don't want to step on myself or get the skis stuck in the snow."

"You'll do both those things and fall over as well," Brandon said. "It's part of the learning curve. I personally prefer skis to snowshoes, although they really are two very different things for different purposes. The best part for me is that after you catch onto the movement, it's second nature, and you can move through the woods almost silently."

They spent the next two hours practicing in Brandon's yard. Riley's excitement and high spirits just intensified Brandon's attraction. Despite pratfalls and some initial awkwardness, Riley took his tumbles good-naturedly, laughing at himself and the "butt prints" he made in the snow and lobbing snowballs at Brandon.

Despite Riley's protests that he wasn't super outdoorsy, he proved a quick learner, and before long, he had the rhythm and movements down well enough that Brandon proclaimed him ready for an easy, flat trail.

Riley beamed as they headed back to the garage. "That was a lot of fun. And you're right—once I got the rhythm, it was a lot easier."

Brandon got out of his skis with practiced ease and then helped Riley. "The skis start to feel like extensions of your feet when you get used to them. You'll learn to get them on and off and how to maneuver better."

"I still step all over myself trying to turn around," Riley admitted. "It's embarrassing."

"Everyone does it—and they all get better at it," Brandon assured him. Riley's cheeks were red from the cold, and he was slightly out of breath, looking absolutely scrumptious.

Back in the house, they stripped off their boots and wet clothing.

Brandon brought out robes for both of them and tossed their clothes in the dryer.

"Since you're nearly naked, stay for lunch," Brandon urged with a wink.

"I'd love to. Thank you for teaching me. It was fun." Riley practically glowed, and Brandon felt struck all over again at his good looks.

"We can go out whenever you want," Brandon offered. "And if you get to the point where you want to buy your own skis, I can go with you and help you make sure they're right for you."

"You know, you might just win me over to this outdoors stuff," Riley teased, accepting a cup of hot coffee and cradling it in his hands, breathing in the hot steam with an ecstatic expression.

Our mate is handsome. Very fuckable.

Brandon choked on his coffee at his moose's observation. He waved off Riley's concern. "Just swallowed wrong."

Riley's phone pinged an alarm, and he sighed. "Unfortunately, I need to run some errands in case the big storm hits this time around."

"The road crews do a good job keeping things clear, but if it comes down too fast, it can get ahead of them," Brandon warned. "And they can't do as much for ice as for snow, so watch out."

Riley nodded. "Steve promised I could stay at the hotel if it got too bad to go home. Which takes a load off my mind. My Pilot is good in snow, but I've never tried driving in a blizzard."

He got dressed, gathered his things, and grabbed his backpack. "I really enjoyed being with you," he told Brandon, meeting his gaze. "And I want to see you again."

Brandon's heart warmed, and he leaned in to kiss Riley slow and long. "I want to see you again too. Real soon. Be careful with the storm."

"I will. You too."

Brandon drove Riley back to where he had parked and helped him clean off his SUV. They took a few more moments to kiss before Riley reached for the door handle.

"I'll see you at your gig," Brandon told him. "I already miss you."

"I was thinking the same thing." Riley added one more peck on the lips. "See you soon."

Brandon stayed until Riley had safely gotten into his Pilot and started it, then watched him pull away.

Damn, I'm utterly smitten.

He's our mate. Of course you are, his moose returned confidently. *So bite him already.*

Brandon sighed in fond exasperation. *I intend to. When the time is right.*

The time is always right to bite your mate.

You're hopeless.

No, I'm your moose, silly.

As he turned around and drove back to the cabin, Brandon hoped that everything would be as simple as his moose predicted.

8

———

RILEY

RILEY SANG ALONG WITH THE RADIO AS HE DROVE, STILL ON A HIGH FROM his time with Brandon. Everything had gone so well, better than Riley dared hope.

We never seem to run out of things to talk about. He isn't annoyed that I'm not super outdoorsy, and he taught me how I can have fun on his turf. We like a lot of the same things. He can cook. And if I had my way, we'd never get out of bed.

Riley touched the hickey on his neck fondly. *Does a mating bite hurt? Will it leave a scar? He'll bite me as a human, I hope. Moose have a lot of teeth.*

Accepting a bite as a declaration of forever love from a moose shifter wasn't what Riley had in mind when he relocated, but now he couldn't imagine being without Brandon.

I'm totally smitten.

Other cars were still on the road, and Riley wondered if they were gathering supplies as well. He hadn't gotten an alert about business closings, but the dark clouds looked forbidding and full of snow.

The music store held down one end of an older strip mall. Riley parked slightly away from other cars, worried about someone sliding into him on the snow. He hurried inside, hoping he could finish his errand, pick up lunch, and get back to the motel with some time to relax before his performance.

And look at job postings. If I'm going to stay, I need something in addition to playing the guitar.

A strange feeling washed over Riley as he walked toward the music store. He stopped and looked around but didn't see anyone nearby. He felt more tired than he expected and chalked it up to the skiing.

Guess I should add a nap to my list before the gig tonight.

Riley checked the prices on some wish list items, found what he was looking for, and took a few minutes to see what else the store carried. By the time he was ready to check out, he felt like he was asleep on his feet. *Wow—skiing must have taken more out of me than I thought.*

"Hope you don't have far to go," the clerk said. "That storm looks like it's coming in faster than they said it might."

Riley glanced outside. Slate gray clouds looked ready to burst with snow. "I don't have far to go. Thanks for the warning."

A gust of wind made Riley shiver. In just an hour, the temperature had fallen, and the sun hid behind the dark clouds. Still, that didn't account for how every step felt leaden, and a sudden headache nearly blurred his vision.

As he reached for the handle of the SUV's door, he felt a hand fall heavy on his shoulder and the muzzle of a gun against his spine.

"We're going home," Tate said, low and menacing. "Taking my car." His pickup truck was parked on the far side of Riley's SUV, and he jabbed Riley with the gun to get him moving in that direction.

"Make noise, and I'll kill you right here." The way their cars were angled, Riley's vehicle hid what was happening from view for most of the lot and anyone in the store.

Panic filled Riley. *Tate found me. He's here. Fuck—he's got a gun. What's he doing to make me like this?*

Brandon! Help!

Riley suddenly felt too tired to keep his eyes open. He saw a glint of metal as the pistol in Tate's hand came up sharply, hitting him in the temple and making the world spin. Blood streamed down the side of his face as consciousness faded.

WHEN HE WOKE, Riley's head pounded, and the left side of his face was sticky with blood. Zip ties bound his wrists and ankles, and a blanket covered him where he was stretched out on the back seat. He spat a rag out of his mouth and took stock. Other than the headache and the damage to his temple, there didn't seem to be any injuries beyond exhaustion.

Tate's a psi-vamp. Guess he only "sipped" before and this time he took big gulps.

I'm not going back with him.

I've got to get loose.

Then he noticed the truck's movement and caught his breath. Tate was driving fast, and the vehicle slipped and slid. Apparently, the snow had started while Riley was unconscious and was coming down thick and heavy.

Idiot. A pickup is terrible in bad snow.

Without much weight over the back wheels, pickups often struggled for traction. Riley knew that Tate had never lived anywhere with worse weather than Jamestown, so his skills in a blizzard weren't likely to be good.

The truck fishtailed wildly. Riley jerked up and lurched forward. "You're going to get us killed!"

"Sit down and shut up," Tate snarled, turning to glare at Riley.

"Watch out!"

Tate turned back to the road seconds too late and hit a patch of ice at full speed. He wrestled with the wheel, overcorrected, and sent the truck spinning.

Riley grabbed the unused backseat shoulder harness, fastening himself in, and braced for impact.

The truck left the road and crashed through the guide rails, thudding down a steep slope with one bone-jarring jolt after another.

Riley saw the tree coming up fast and tucked himself down in a crash position.

I love you, Brandon. Sorry I never got to tell you.

Please find my body so you know I didn't leave on purpose.

Remember me.

The truck hit the tree head-on. Tate flew forward through the windshield in a spray of blood.

Riley's seatbelt locked, catching him hard enough to bruise, then the impact threw him back into the headrest. His vision swam, and for the second time, he blacked out.

When he came around, Riley smelled blood and gasoline. *Always a bad combination.*

Tate lay across the crumpled hood of the truck, bloody and still.

Riley moved gingerly, testing to see if he had any broken bones. His ribs hurt like a muther, his head pounded, and he could taste blood in his mouth where he had bitten his cheek, but his arms and legs seemed okay, although the damn zip ties still held.

"One thing at a time." He managed to unfasten the shoulder harness. The back seat was littered with broken glass, and he rubbed his ties against a shard that was still in the side window, freeing his hands. Another shard cut his ankles free.

Riley took stock. *They tell you to stay with the wreck—unless it might explode. I don't know where I am, but I'm betting Tate took the highway toward Jamestown. The storm's hitting, so sane people won't be on the road. Maybe road crews—and maybe not.*

If anyone comes looking for me, they'll never find me down here. Not with the way the snow is falling. We'll get covered.

He realized that the blanket that had covered him was red. He grabbed it and hunted for his phone and wallet. Riley found them up front. The wallet lay in the center section, and he grabbed it and put it back in his pocket. His phone was broken from the impact. Tate's phone was nowhere to be seen.

Riley made a quick search for an emergency kit, hoping to find flares. He found nothing in the cab, and the keys to the box in the bed of the pickup were probably on Tate's body, which he was not about to touch.

Tate hadn't taken Riley's coat or boots, but he had removed his own coat, which lay on the front seat. Riley grabbed it, knowing that he was going to need all the insulation he could get.

The smell of gas seemed stronger. Riley's door had jammed, so he knocked out the rest of the broken glass and managed to wriggle through. The effort made his head swim, so he had to rest before he could leave the wreck.

Dark clouds hid the sun and gave him no way to navigate. Snow had already partially obscured the tracks down the slope but gave him hope of a direction. *Unless we completely spun around and were moving opposite traffic when we went down the slope.*

Can't stay, and no one will find me down here, so I'd better start climbing.

Riley might not have broken any bones in the crash, but everything hurt. He picked his way up the slope, watching his footing carefully. Twice he slid back several feet when snow-covered rocks shifted under his weight. The road seemed so high above him, unreachable, but he kept going, one step at a time, gritting his teeth against the pain.

How long will it take before they notice I'm missing?

Riley fought through the snow, panting from exertion and pain. He could feel how drained he was from Tate's psi-vamp trick, something that his ex had either learned since they broke up or that he had never felt the need to use full force on Riley before.

The enhanced fatigue meant Riley might not get much farther than back to the road. He couldn't hear any cars going by. With how thick and fast the snow was coming down, he wondered if the road was closed.

After what seemed forever, he dragged himself over the mangled guide rail, leaving a bloody handprint. The twisted steel would soon be the only clue to his passing since snow was filling in the tire tracks on the road and down over the slope.

At least I'm not close if the truck blows up. That could be a good thing to attract attention—if anyone is looking.

Riley covered his mouth with his scarf as he struggled to catch his breath. His mittens and jeans were soaked. Tate's coat was tied around his waist, and he had stuffed the red blanket inside his parka to keep it dry. On a whim, he had also grabbed the rear-view mirror that dangled from the shards of the windshield and shoved it in a pocket, still trailing wires.

No one is going to be out in this—maybe not even the plows if they close the road.

I'm in the middle of nowhere, no one knows I'm missing, it's cold and snowing, I'm hurt, and I've got no way to call for help. There's no reason anyone should think to look for me here.

I'm probably not getting out of this alive.

Riley couldn't see any traffic in either direction. From the rapidly filling tracks, it looked like Tate had gone into a spin, torn across the median, skidded through the guide rail on the opposite side of traffic, and then gone down over the embankment.

He shuddered, realizing how lucky he was to be alive and relatively unhurt.

Then again, bleeding out is faster than freezing to death.

A bitter gust knifed past him. Even if he hadn't been drained and injured, the frigid temperature and deep snow would do him in long before he made it to the next exit.

I need to get out of the elements.

He eyed the mountain of snow in the median pushed there by the last snow plow. It had glazed with the wind, making a rigid pile. Nearby, a heap of road junk peeked from beneath the snow.

I can make a snow cave if any of that junk is hard enough to let me chip out the icy top layer so I can get shelter from the wind.

It won't save my life if someone doesn't find me soon, but it might buy me a little time.

His remaining energy was fading fast, and the aching muscles from the wreck were starting to stiffen up. Riley set to his task, resolutely ignoring the headache that made him grit his teeth and grimace at the pain. A broken piece of two-by-four was the best implement he could find in the junk pile, but it was enough to carve a shallow indentation just deep enough for his body with a slight overhang to blunt the wind.

Riley pushed Tate's coat in first to insulate him from the snow. He shoved the broken two-by-four into a smaller drift and used the tangle of wires to tie the rearview mirror to the wood, hoping that the reflected light would attract a rescuer. Then Riley crawled into the snow cave, using the red blanket as the final layer of insulation, hoping the bright color might attract attention or the mirror reflecting headlights would draw a rescuer.

Those were both long shots, he admitted, getting as comfortable as he could, huddled in the makeshift shelter. Riley covered his face with his scarf and tucked his hands into his armpits. His parka covered his front as did the red blanket, while Tate's coat kept him from lying against the snow.

Long ago, he had read an article about hypothermia. Riley was shivering, and his teeth chattered, but he knew that was a good sign. *If the shivering stops…it's bad.*

When he didn't show up for his gig, Todd would make calls. Brandon and Dr. Jeffries would sound the alarm. Rescuers would mobilize. And by then, it would be too late.

Resigned, Riley turned to his imagination for comfort.

Brandon and I barely got to start…and now it'll be over. I imagine the sheriff will piece together what happened once they find the wreck.

I didn't get to tell Brandon that I love him, whether or not we're true mates. If he really is a moose shifter, I didn't get to see his moose or accept his bite. Will it harm him to lose his mate?

I wanted more time together. I wanted forever.

Is a true mate's death something a shifter doesn't get over?

Riley closed his eyes and pictured the future he would never see. Laughing with Brandon as they moved him into the cabin. Toasting marshmallows over the fireplace. Making love by the fire's glow. Cooking meals together. Watching the trees bud in the spring and seeing the forest come to life. Come summer, swimming in the lake or taking a canoe out on the water.

Riley imagined how the mountains must glow in autumn and thought about going for long walks amid falling leaves. Decorating a Christmas tree together and exchanging gifts in front of the fire. Growing older, year by year, hand in hand. He wouldn't experience any of those moments, but it comforted him to imagine them.

Fated mates and a perfect zodiac match. We would have been so good together. He'd never liked being alone with his thoughts for too long—

another Gemini thing—but now thoughts, memories, and regrets were all he had.

Riley knew he should fight the exhaustion that swept over him, that falling asleep out here would be deadly, but he lacked the energy to struggle. He hoped hypothermia was as peaceful a death as stories made it out to be.

His eyelids kept drifting shut no matter how hard he fought, heavy with sleep. *Time to let go.*

Loud crashing and bellowing woke him with a start. It sounded like a freight train was barreling toward him, blaring an air raid siren.

Riley opened his eyes and drew back the red blanket. A massive bull moose thundered toward him, hurtling through the deep snow as if it was bare ground. Huge antlers stood out against the gray sky. The very loud noise was coming from the moose, like an amplified air horn.

Brandon?

Riley struggled to move, grabbing the red blanket and waving it as best he could. "Brandon!" he shouted. "Over here!"

The moose's huge head swung toward him, and the creature's nose twitched. It slowed its pace, scenting the air, and then made straight for Riley's snow cave. Just in front of his shelter, the moose knelt and pushed its nose toward him, taking a deep inhale.

"Brandon?" Riley reached out a shaking hand and gently stroked the bridge of the moose's nose. It blinked in response. Riley realized the moose wore something around its neck on a sturdy collar and saw that it was a tracking device.

"Thank you for coming for me." He struggled to speak, slurring his words. "I love you. I wanted to be your mate. I'm sorry we won't get time."

The moose made a pitiful sound and started to shift position. Inch by inch, the huge animal maneuvered its sizeable bulk until it blocked the door to the snow cave with its body, surprisingly careful not to squash Riley.

In just moments, the moose's body heat warmed the cave. Riley reached out to pet the thick neck with gentle strokes.

"I'm glad you're here," Riley whispered. "I didn't want to die alone."

The moose's distressed noise conveyed its worry and fear.

Riley couldn't fight the exhaustion any longer, but the scent of the moose calmed him, reminded him of where he belonged. "Mate," he sighed, wrapping his arm around the moose's neck.

As he lost consciousness, he thought he heard the roar of motors growing louder, but then again, it might have been the wind.

9

BRANDON

HE WATCHED THE STORM CLOUDS GROW DARK AND WISHED RILEY HADN'T
needed to leave.

*We could have spent the day in front of the fireplace, finding ways to stay
warm.*

It's a bad day for our mate to be out.

I can't tell him that he's not allowed to go.

Humans, his moose huffed in annoyance and withdrew.

Brandon gathered towels for laundry and stripped the bed, pleased
that he could still catch Riley's scent on the sheets. He pondered what
to make for dinner and wondered if the hotel would cancel Riley's gig
that night. From the way the snow was coming down, odds were high
that everything would close early—and some roads would close
altogether.

The Adirondacks knew how to handle heavy snow. Brandon had
heard the distant rumble of the big trucks that would plow and salt the
main roads. People who lived in Fox Hollow year-round got by with
snowplows, snowblowers, snow shoes, skis, all-wheel drive, and sheer
stubbornness.

Will the storm scare Riley off? This weather isn't for everyone, and he doesn't have a shifter side to compensate. Jamestown doesn't get this much snow. It definitely is an acquired taste unless your animal side is born to it.

It hadn't been long since he and Riley had gotten together, but Brandon knew he was already in love. Part of that was the fated mates from his shifter side, but human Brandon had fallen head over heels as well.

They would have to have "the talk" soon, before things went any further. That wasn't an issue with a shifter partner because they could sense the other's dual nature.

He wondered if Riley suspected. Since Riley knew Madden and Madden had a penchant for gossip—nothing malicious, but he was the go-to person for local news—Brandon thought Riley might be waiting for the right time to bring it up.

By the way, are you a moose? They don't cover that kind of thing in dating tips articles.

Brandon sighed. He wondered if the feeling of *belonging* was as strong for a human as it was for a shifter. To Brandon, that certainty of finding his true mate eased the awkwardness of getting to know each other, knowing that they were meant to be together and that everything would work out.

He knew from his mated and married friends that fated mates still had to work on their relationship, but the mate bond went a long way toward avoiding many of the irritations that arose in non-shifter partnerships.

As his other friends found their mates, Brandon had wondered when it would be his turn. He wasn't exactly lonely surrounded by a close group of friends and deep in the active Fox Hollow community, but he longed for someone of his own. When he caught Riley's scent and realized this could be his mate, Brandon realized just how much he wanted to find the right person.

Riley seemed to be completely on board with the idea. There was a lot they hadn't talked about yet, moose notwithstanding, but despite the quick intensity of their bond, they still hadn't been together long. *He's getting used to a new town, new job, and new classes at the Institute. There hasn't been a lot of time for heart-to-hearts just yet. If we're true mates, that will happen.*

Bite him and fuck him. That goes a long way toward "communicating," his moose pointed out. *You might be able to read more from him through a mate bond than usual with his whole freaky nil thing.*

Being a nil isn't "freaky." It's part of who he is, and a legitimate psychic gift, Brandon defended. *And it's nice that I'm not bombarded with thoughts for once. I don't have to shield. I can just be me, and he doesn't have to worry that I'm rustling through his mental "drawers."*

Whatever you say, his moose snarked.

A weather alert blared on Brandon's phone, and he glanced at the screen. *Six-to-eight-inch accumulation over the next hour, with more likely. Dangerous wind chill. Roads closed to all but emergency traffic. Businesses closing. Shelter livestock; bring pets inside. Stay off the roads.*

The "snowmageddon" everyone had been predicting was late, but it finally showed up and demanded attention. Brandon had already split extra wood for the fire, stocked up on food, and made sure there was gas for the generator.

Now if only Riley had decided to stay. He's not going to be playing tonight since everything is closing. It would have been more fun to be snowed in together.

Between one breath and the next, blinding pain hit Brandon hard enough to drive him to his knees. His head pounded, his heart raced with terror, and he heard Riley scream his name.

"What the fuck was that?" Brandon sat on the floor of the kitchen holding his head.

Our mate is in danger! his moose roared.

Brandon shook his head to clear it. He might not be able to read Riley in the same way as his regular telepathy, but their mate bond made some level of connection possible—and right now, Riley was scared, hurt, and in danger.

He was going to pick up new strings and go back to the motel, maybe catch a nap before his gig tonight—which is going to be canceled, given the storm.

Did he wreck in the snow?

Brandon called Riley's phone and listened as it rang until the call went to voicemail. He tried again, without result.

He began to pace in the kitchen. His telepathy usually didn't work over long distances, even with someone who was an easy read. Given the intensity of the emotions he picked up from Riley, Brandon knew it had to be the mate bond connecting them, which was why he read feelings and not words. But even without language, the terror and danger were viscerally clear.

His moose and his Aries nature were in complete agreement on a fierce protective streak.

I've got to find him.

Our mate needs us, his moose demanded.

He jumped when his phone rang. A glance at the screen told him it wasn't Riley, and it took a moment to register it was from Madden.

"Brandon! Code Red! I think Riley's been kidnapped!" Madden's voice had gone up a few notes in excitement, and he spoke so fast Brandon had to listen closely to catch all the words.

"Slow down and say that again. Kidnapped?"

"I saw it. Some guy pushed him into a truck and took off. I already called the sheriff, and I'm heading to the fire department to rally our friends."

Brandon shook his head, trying to make sense of Madden's garbled account. "Okay, I'm still not following. Why would anyone kidnap Riley?"

"His ex. From Jamestown. He's some sort of stalker. Steve at the motel told me that Riley put security cameras up, and Steve was trying to figure out whether to let him keep them. Riley filed a restraining order with the sheriff when he moved here."

"Does everyone in town tell you what's going on?'

"Yes. Of course they do."

Riley has a stalker ex. He never told me that part. Then again, maybe he thought I'd think less of him for some reason. They're history. It wouldn't have mattered to me anyway—we'll make a fresh start of our own.

Pay attention! Someone has taken our mate! In his mind, his inner moose pawed at the dirt and shook his antlers in challenge, ready to fight.

Brandon looked out the window. Heavy, wet snow fell so thick Brandon could barely see. The wind had picked up, driving the loose snow into drifts.

"They aren't going to get far in this weather," Brandon said. "And we've got wolves and a beagle shifter who can track scent." Except that if Riley was in a truck, he wouldn't leave a scent. And he could be anywhere.

Riley came here from Jamestown. It makes sense that's where his stalker would take him.

"Madden—how long ago did this happen?"

"About fifteen minutes since I called the sheriff first. I was going to call Russ and Drew and the others next." Two wolves, a bobcat, a lynx, a fox, and a squirrel were an unlikely rescue squad, but Brandon would bet on them any day.

Brandon took a deep breath, trying to clear his thoughts and make a plan. "What kind of truck?"

"A blue pickup."

A pickup wouldn't get anywhere fast in this snow, Brandon thought.

Riley's out in that storm with a madman. Anyone crazy enough to kidnap their ex might do worse.

The kidnapper is probably going to try to go back to Jamestown. He won't make it in this weather.

The back roads will be impassible. He'll have to stick to the highway—and it's not likely to be open for long.

Good thing I'm an all-terrain moose.

"I'm going after him," Brandon told Madden. "I think they'll stick to the main highway, heading toward Jamestown. Tell the sheriff I'm going to wear my tracker—and break out the snowmobiles to follow me."

"I'm on it. Good luck."

Brandon forced his fear down and focused on what he could do to protect Riley. He didn't fault his boyfriend for not telling him about a crazy ex. They had only just become a couple, and Riley probably wanted to leave the ugly past behind him. Brandon hadn't shared all his secrets, either.

He had assisted with winter search and rescues before and kept his gear in a closet, ready to go. Brandon decided to take the bag with his equipment in the SUV and wear the tracker so the sheriff could find him…hopefully once he had found Riley.

As for the stalker ex, moose-Brandon was thirteen hundred pounds of muscle. He knew how to take care of himself.

Brandon channeled his worry for Riley into action and forced himself to think strategically. Even in deep snow, his moose could move at a top speed of about forty miles per hour—faster than four-wheel drives were likely to go in this storm. His gear bag had survival equipment and first aid materials, energy bars, and sports drinks, but carrying it would slow Brandon down, and in the biting cold, that could cost time Riley didn't have. He would need to leave the bag in his SUV and hope that he could find Riley and lead the others to him.

Too many "ifs," he fretted.

Brandon loaded his gear into the Suburban as well as the tracker harness that the sheriff had specially made for him. He dressed for the weather with his warmest coat, boots, hat, and gloves, but Brandon knew he wouldn't get far in the vehicle given the storm.

He'd go as far as he could in the SUV, then shift and do the rest in his fur and hope he could get to Riley before something terrible happened.

Snow crunched under his wheels, and Brandon could feel the drag on his tires as he made his way down unplowed roads. It was coming down faster than the road crew could clear it, something that didn't happen often in Fox Hollow but wasn't unheard of for a storm of the year.

Everyone else had apparently gotten the message to stay home because the roads were empty. Snow rapidly blurred old tracks. Even with the four-wheel drive engaged, Brandon could feel the tires strain for grip in slick spots.

Riley's ex had taken him in a pickup. Trying to drive a truck without a load in the back for traction was suicidal. All the weight was in the engine, not over the back wheels, making it difficult if not impossible to control.

Maybe they'll get stuck. I can catch up to them if they're stranded.

Does his ex have a gun? Probably. I'll have to take my chances that the asshole isn't a moose hunter.

Brandon knew he wasn't bulletproof as a moose. A high-caliber rifle or handgun would be enough to kill him, along with any automatic weapon. A smaller gun might get in a lucky shot. Then again, if the bullet didn't hit anything vital, it could be like trying to stop a moving train.

He wasn't surprised to find the turn to the main state route blocked with safety barriers. Brandon pulled off to the side of the road and started to strip off clothing and boots. Shifting would be damned uncomfortable, but saving Riley was worth it.

Although he'll be annoyed if I freeze my dangly bits—and so will I.

The specially-made tracker harness was designed so he could get into it once he had shifted since nothing would fit when he made the change. The antlers added an extra challenge, but with practice, he'd learned how to duck into it and cinch the straps with his teeth.

Bracing himself for the chill, Brandon got out of the SUV and hung the harness from the outside mirror. Even using the vehicle as a windbreak, Brandon shivered violently as he waited for the shift to take hold.

Once he was in moose form, warmth wasn't a problem. He nudged the door shut, very carefully angled his antlers, and eased his head through the tracker's strap, then bit the end and pulled it tight. Locking the SUV wasn't a possibility with hooves, but no one was going to be around to steal it today.

Brandon stepped away from the vehicle and shook his antlers, then lifted his head and scented the wind. His eyesight as a moose was poor, but hearing and smell went a long way to make up for the lack.

No tire tracks were visible, not surprising considering the wind and fast accumulation. That also meant no noises or smells to confuse his senses.

What if he didn't go this way? his moose fretted.

His ex wasn't from around here. He doesn't know back ways, and with the storm, he'd be likely to stick to the big road.

If you're wrong, how can we find him? It might be too late.

Brandon shut down that train of thought. He couldn't afford to believe that Riley was beyond saving. *Madden is going to get the rescue crew. They might be able to get a license plate from the traffic cams leaving the plaza. Not that I think they got very far.*

The best he could hope for would be to find the truck stuck in the snow. He refused to let himself imagine worse scenarios.

Brandon started at a brisk walk, and once he had a feel for the road, he worked up to a full run. He couldn't keep top speed for long, but he could maintain a slightly slower speed for quite a while.

Please be safe. Please don't die. Please hang on.

I'm coming for you. I love you. I need my mate.

Please wait for me.

The first couple of miles passed without spotting tracks or a stalled car. No vehicles were on the road, giving it an apocalyptic feel. Brandon tried to quell his fear and push down panic, but doubts began to surface despite his efforts.

What if I guessed wrong about the route? What if they went a different way? Maybe they got out of Fox Hollow and holed up at a hotel. All the towns are going to be focused on clearing roads, helping stranded motorists, and dealing with emergencies. A manhunt is going to be a low priority.

Once Madden gets the rescue effort going, they'll check area hotels and put out a BOLO so any emergency responders who are out will be alert. We'll find him. We have to.

Still, Brandon's gut told him this was the most likely route. Between the wind and the heavy snow, the road looked untouched.

Then he spotted the mangled guide rail. *It's on the other side. They weren't going that direction. That would be back toward Fox Hollow.*

But what if they lost control?

Brandon could see how it could happen. The ex-boyfriend, driving too fast to put Fox Hollow behind them and unfamiliar with how to drive in a true blizzard. All it would take would be hitting ice to send a pickup skidding.

He veered and charged across the deserted lanes for a closer look. The guide rail had been torn loose, and once he reached the edge of the roadway, Brandon could see that a vehicle had gone down over the side until it hit a tree.

He listened for movement and heard only the wind. His keen nose smelled gasoline—and blood. Brandon picked his way down the slope unimpeded by the snow. His heart sank when he saw a blue pickup crumpled against the thick trunk of a tall oak.

Brandon edged closer. He caught a whiff of his mate's scent, but not as strong as he expected. The blood smell grew more prominent as he got closer, as well as the smell of an unfamiliar human.

Then he saw the rest of the damage to the truck. All the side windows were broken out, the front end was badly smashed, and the driver had been thrown through the windshield. That's when Brandon spotted the corpse on the hood, buried beneath new-fallen snow.

Frightened to see but needing to know, Brandon moved up to the front of the wreck and poked the body with his antlers. It didn't move, and he could tell from its odor that the stranger was dead.

Where's Riley?

Brandon saw the broken rear windows and spotted smears of blood on some of the shards, but he couldn't see Riley in or near the truck. Making a careful circle, he saw a depression in the snow that might have been tracks nearly filled in by new accumulation.

Trying not to panic, Brandon followed the shallow trough up the embankment. It cut upward at a slant, instead of going directly to the top.

Logical if Riley was hurt or had trouble climbing. Please let him be okay.

Brandon reached the top of the slope a few yards from where he had descended. He stood on the empty road and looked around, desperate to catch sight of Riley.

I don't know which way he went. Toward Jamestown — or back toward Fox Hollow? Did he even know where he was since the truck got turned around?

A bright flash caught his eye. A large snow pile sat in the median where plows had pushed their loads. The broken rearview mirror dangled in the wind from a two-by-four, reflecting the sun.

Brandon bellowed as loudly as he could to tell his mate he was on the way and began running at full speed. He crashed through the snow effortlessly, long legs eating up the distance.

Just as he got close, Riley spotted him, waving and shouting.

"Brandon! Over here!"

I guess he figured out the moose part, Brandon's other side said. *Go save our mate.*

Riley's scent was much stronger now, mingled with blood. Brandon slowed and approached the snow cave cautiously, not wanting to make it collapse. He knelt in front of the opening and pushed his nose inside.

"Brandon?" Riley reached toward him and stroked his face. His hand shook, and his whole body shivered violently.

"Thank you for coming for me." Riley sounded drugged or sleepy. "I love you. I wanted to be your mate. I'm sorry we won't get time."

Brandon raised his head and let out a mournful bellow. *I don't dare shift, or we'll both die from exposure. But maybe I can make it better until help arrives.*

His tracker would alert the emergency team to where he was, and when he stopped moving, they would know he had found Riley. He just needed to keep Riley alive until the rescuers caught up.

Very carefully, Brandon shifted his huge bulk until his body blocked the entrance to the snow cave. That meant putting his back to Riley when he desperately wanted to see his mate, but he knew it would keep him warmer.

"I'm glad you're here," Riley whispered. "I didn't want to die alone."

Riley's words broke Brandon's heart, and his moose huffed a response.

Riley settled in behind Brandon, lying close, and slipped an arm around as much of the huge animal as he could reach.

"Mate." Riley sighed, and then fell quiet.

Brandon snuffled, but Riley didn't answer.

He couldn't hear Riley's thoughts, but the emotions he sensed ranged from fear to acceptance, and from Riley's scent, Brandon could tell his mate was fading.

He's dying, Brandon's moose said, sounding as heartbroken as human Brandon felt. *Save him.*

He's too weak to ride us. We can't carry him out. The tracker will bring help. Brandon's feelings careened between terror and grief, afraid that he had still arrived too late.

A distant hum made Brandon's ears prick up. *Snowmobiles. They're coming.*

Top speed for a moose could hit forty miles per hour, but a snow-mobile could do over one hundred. They could get Riley to the hospital faster and more safely, and Brandon would catch up to them.

Two snowmobiles roared up and stopped a few feet from where Brandon lay. He maneuvered carefully to avoid squashing Riley, getting out of the way.

"Great job, Brandon," Russ said as he and Noah got off one of the snowmobiles. "You found him."

"We'll get him to the hospital," Drew added as he dismounted from the second snowmobile, which had a rescue sled.

Riley didn't rouse when Russ and Drew tried to wake him, so they eased him from the snow cave and carried him to the sled. Noah grabbed the blanket and extra coat to tuck around Riley to keep him as warm as possible on the way back to town.

"We'll take good care of him." Noah met Brandon's gaze. "I promise."

Brandon got back to his feet and watched as they roared away. His body didn't mind the cold, but his heart felt frozen solid.

We could lose our mate. His inner moose sounded sorrowful.

We're going to do everything we can to save him. Even as Brandon promised, he didn't know what more he could do to make that vow come true.

The trek back to his SUV seemed to take forever, even though Brandon kept the fastest, steady pace he could sustain. His moose side stayed unusually quiet, brooding. Brandon's long legs ate up the snowy road, getting him back to where he had parked in record time.

Snow covered the Suburban, several inches deep just in the time he had been gone. He dreaded shifting because the wind had picked up but endured the bitter cold and threw himself into the vehicle as soon as he could get the door open.

"Cold, cold, so fuckin' cold." He scrambled to pull on his clothes and coat, wondering if his skin would freeze to the upholstery.

Brandon started the SUV and blasted the heat, fairly certain it wouldn't warm up before he got to his destination. He shut off the radio, in no mood for distractions. All he cared about was getting to the hospital to be with Riley, and that meant being cautious so he didn't end up in a wreck of his own.

He breathed a sigh of relief when he got back to town and saw that the plows had cleared at least some of the snow from the main road, although with the way it was still coming down, that wouldn't last long.

Brandon parked at the Emergency Room, grabbed his backpack, and ran inside.

"Where's Riley?" he asked Tricia, one of the nurses he recognized behind the desk. "The car wreck case the sheriff just brought in."

"Hi, Brandon. They said you'd be along. He's in with the doctor right now. I'll let you know when you can see him. Go ahead and get comfortable in the waiting room. There's coffee."

Brandon thanked her and took a chair. Restless, he got up and made coffee from the single-serve machine, then tried to settle into his seat. While his moose had been fine in the cold, he still wasn't over the chill from shifting, and only now did he feel the fatigue.

He dug a protein bar out of his backpack and gobbled it, washing it down with a sports drink and then the coffee. Still hungry, he ate two more before realizing that the empty pit in his stomach was probably more from worry than hunger at this point.

"Brandon."

He looked up and saw Russ coming toward him, wearing his EMT uniform.

"How is he?" Brandon blurted. He knew Riley had been in rough shape, but he couldn't bring himself to question aloud whether or not he was still alive.

Russ came and sat next to him. "The doctor's with him now. Hypothermia and exposure, a concussion, and some bad bruises and cuts."

"There was a wreck," Brandon told him. "The kidnapper's truck must have spun out, got turned the other way, crossed the median and the opposite lanes, and went down the embankment. The driver got thrown out of the windshield—he was dead. I can lead you to the scene if you need me to."

"Later," Russ said. "I don't think anyone is going to bother it until the storm is over, and even the scavengers will steer clear until the storm ends."

Brandon shivered, remembering his fear until he confirmed that the body wasn't Riley.

"Madden was going to spearhead finding out who the guy was. Any luck?"

Russ shook his head. "We went out right after you did. I imagine the sheriff will want to talk to you. And if he won't tell you anything, Madden will," he added with a smirk.

Drew and Noah joined them, adding words of encouragement before they had to head out to deal with other emergencies. That left Brandon alone in the waiting room.

He glanced at his phone and saw he had a message from Madden. He returned the call, and Madden picked up on the first ring.

"Brandon! Did you find him? Is he okay?"

"I found him. Whether or not he's okay, I don't know yet. There was a wreck, he's hurt, he got away, but he was out in the cold—he wasn't in good shape when I found him." Brandon couldn't hold his worry inside any longer.

"Are you at the E.R.? I can come sit with you if you need company."

Brandon's heart warmed at the offer, but he knew he had to decline. "Stay home with Elias where it's safe. Russ and the others just went back to work. I'll get to see Riley when the doctors are done with him. I don't know that they'll tell me much since we don't have an official relationship."

"You do know that being fated mates counts as 'official' in Fox Hollow," Madden said.

"It does?"

"Yep. Do you have a mating bite?"

"Um—what about a mating hickey? We were working up to the bite part."

"I think that will do, given the circumstances," Madden replied, barely keeping from laughing.

"Thanks, Madden. For everything."

"Hey, it's what we do here. Keep me posted."

Brandon felt lonely when the call ended, too restless to sit still and too exhausted from the rescue to pace. He ate a chocolate bar from his pack and made a second cup of coffee before dropping heavily into his chair.

Games and social media on his phone didn't hold his attention, and nothing distracted from his worry. Riley had been prepared to die. *Are we over before we even got a chance to start?*

He had never been more grateful for the company of his inner moose. He and his other half consoled each other just by being present together. For once, his moose's snark was gone, replaced by somber silence.

"Brandon Davis?"

Brandon looked up to see a woman in a white coat in the doorway of the waiting room. He stood. "That's me. Riley's my fated mate. How is he?"

The doctor smiled. "I've never seen a mating hickey before."

"We were working up to an actual bite, but we've both acknowledged that we have a mating bond," Brandon replied. "Please, tell me if he made it or not." He usually had strict boundaries about reading minds, but he was sorely tempted to break the rules in his panic over Riley.

She gestured toward the seats, and they sat down facing each other. "I'm Dr. Swanson. Riley is alive—and he's going to stay that way."

Brandon whooshed out a long breath. "That's good. That's real good. How bad is he hurt?"

She frowned. "He was in a car wreck?"

"His crazy ex kidnapped him and then skidded off the road and hit a tree," Brandon said. "That's all I know."

"He has bruising consistent with a shoulder and lap belt in a crash, as well lacerations that look like they came from broken glass. I'm not sure how the concussion happened."

"A witness said the kidnapper struck him."

Dr. Swanson nodded. "That's a possibility. We've treated the exposure and are bringing his body temperature back up. There's no frostbite, so that's positive. It's the concussion that has me worried. He hasn't woken."

Brandon's heart sank. "Is that normal?"

She grimaced. "Normal is a range, not a number. It's not uncommon to be unconscious for anywhere from three to twenty-four hours after a concussion, although anything beyond that is a signal of bigger problems. We did scans, and the images look good. I don't see any bleeding."

"That's good, right?"

"Yes. And remaining unconscious can be the mind and body's way of forcing rest. Especially if there were traumatic events leading up to the injury. Riley may need to heal before he's ready to deal with the aftermath."

"Can I stay with him? I promise I won't be any trouble."

She gave him a compassionate glance. "You look like you've had a rough time of it yourself. Let me guess—you shifted fast and pushed yourself hard. Right?"

Brandon had heard of shifters experiencing a backlash if they forced themselves to shift too fast or too often. "Maybe."

"Moose shifter?" she asked, and he wondered what type she was.

"Yeah. How'd you guess?"

"The big ones have more trouble with quick shifts than the smaller animals. Still not a good idea for the littler ones to switch back and forth fast, but they don't seem to get the same 'whiplash' that the larger animals do."

"Makes sense."

"Have you eaten a meal since you shifted?"

Brandon gave a guilty shake of his head. *Busted.*

"I'll make you a deal." Dr. Swanson smiled. "Go eat a real dinner— our cafeteria here is pretty good—and then you can stay with him as long as you want. Fated mate privilege."

"Thank you." His stomach rumbled. "I didn't want to miss hearing how he was, and until I knew, I didn't think I could keep anything down. Now, I'm starving."

"I'll even see if they can put a recliner in the room so you can spend the night." She put a hand on Brandon's arm. "I really think he's going to be okay. Hang on to that."

Brandon ate as quickly as he could, eager to be with Riley. The food was better than he expected from a hospital cafeteria, and he was famished from exertion, but he couldn't enjoy the meal without seeing for himself that Riley was okay.

Dr. Swanson was in the hallway when he returned to the E.R. and waved him over. "You can see Riley now. He's in 403. He's not awake yet, but talking to him quietly is good. We know that patients can often hear what's said around them even when they're not awake. So, tell him positive things and give him a reason to wake up."

He thanked her and hurried to find Riley's room, then hesitated just outside the door.

What are you waiting for? Our mate is hurt.

I guess I'm afraid that it'll be worse than I think.

Being with our mate is good for healing. We can share our energy. Go to him.

Brandon took a deep breath and opened the door. Riley lay pale and unmoving on the bed, hooked up to monitors. Bandages wound around one side of his head, and he had a black eye. Gauze on his hands looked more like coverings for cuts than treatment for frostbite.

Riley had so much natural energy that seeing him still seemed utterly wrong. Brandon closed his eyes and choked back a sob.

I've got to be positive for him.

He needs us, his moose prompted.

Brandon saw that a recliner had been moved into the room. He pulled a smaller chair up to Riley's bedside and blinked to keep tears at bay.

"I'm here. I love you. Please, be okay." Brandon sat next to Riley's bed and took Riley's hand in both of his.

"You're our mate. We're meant to be together. Rest and get better, and then come back to me. We have so much to do together."

Riley gave no indication of having heard Brandon's pleas. Brandon stared at the monitors as if they could reveal the meaning of life. Some were familiar, others less so. He felt bewildered.

"I'm going to stay right here," Brandon told him. "They're going to let me sleep in the room with you. That's good—because they shut everything down.

"There's so much snow out there. And you found a way to get a snowmobile ride before I could go with you, didn't you?" Brandon tried to tease Riley, but his voice choked.

"If I know Madden, he's got everyone in town signing up to bring casseroles once you get out of here. He saved your life. Saw what happened in the parking lot, called the sheriff, and then called me."

Brandon wiped away his tears with the back of his hand. "If it wasn't for Madden, we wouldn't have known what happened to you. You'd have just vanished…and I wouldn't have found you. So we owe him, big time."

He reached for a tissue from the box on the nightstand. "I found the truck—and your kidnapper. He's dead. You don't have to worry about him anymore. God, Riley, you don't know how much I just wanted to trample everything; I was so scared and furious. And let me tell you, that pickup wouldn't have stood a chance by the time I was done with it."

He looked for some hint that Riley had heard, but Riley's face remained placid.

"I know it's still early for us. We've got a lot to learn about each other. That might get easier when I actually bite you, but even if it doesn't, we'll manage," Brandon continued. "I want you to move in with me. Build a future. Be together forever."

He dabbed at his eyes and cleared his throat. "I'm glad you got to meet my moose, although the circumstances sucked. He's rather handsome if I do say so myself. He says you smell like anise and maple—that's how we knew you were our mate. It's my new favorite scent." He forced a smile despite his tears.

"I'm going to stay here and ramble until you wake up, so don't make me wait forever because I'll end up saying my multiplication tables after a while," Brandon said.

"I think about how things can be for us before I fall asleep. You'll take your classes and play music, maybe find a side job. We'll trip over each other in the cabin for a while, but we'll figure it out eventually. We'll laugh and have sweaty sex. I'll go to hear you play, and you'll go on a tour with me once in a while. We'll get old together."

Brandon had to stop to get control of his emotions and clear his throat. "I want that future so bad, Riley. I want you. But to make it happen, you have to wake up, babe. I'll be here, waiting. Just please—don't make me wait too long."

Brandon had run out of words. He pulled a bottle of water out of his backpack and eased his parched throat. Riley hadn't stirred.

"When I think of something else to say, I'll bore you some more." He laced his fingers with Riley's. "I'm not going anywhere. Just—please come back to me."

10

RILEY

HE REMEMBERED THE MOOSE.

Just when Riley had been certain his luck had run out, a huge black moose came barreling toward him making an incredibly loud noise. It was the strangest thing he'd ever seen, and if he hadn't been so cold, he would have wondered if he was already dead.

When the moose laid down and pushed its huge nose into his snow cave to snuffle him, Riley had no doubts that this was Brandon, his moose mate. Except Riley was also pretty sure he wasn't going to make it, and the thought of leaving Brandon made him sadder than just the idea of dying.

He remembered the loud rumble of engines and losing the heat of his moose protector as he was manhandled into a sled and whisked away. Riley had drifted in and out of consciousness, but when he did open his eyes, the scenery flew by at an alarming pace, and the moose was nowhere to be seen.

His head hurt so much. At some point on the journey, Riley gave up and let sleep take him, hoping the pain would go away.

Riley faded in and out. He heard voices in the distance. Some he knew; most he didn't. They sounded worried, but he didn't have the energy to care. He knew a voice was missing, an important voice, but his thoughts were too muddled to know whose.

The cold was gone, and the air smelled of disinfectant. He was warm. Everything hurt. The pounding in his head hadn't stopped, but once in a while, he could surface, although he couldn't seem to make himself do anything. Riley wondered where Brandon had gone. Then he quit struggling and sank into sleep.

The next time he roused, Brandon was talking to him, gripping his hand. Riley couldn't think clearly, but he felt the pain in Brandon's voice. He wished Brandon could read his mind or that he could give his mate a signal that he could hear him, but his body wasn't cooperating.

Brandon's soothing voice tethered Riley, comforting him. The words slipped past him, not quite registering, but the tone was loving and reassuring. He knew Brandon was hurting, but he couldn't answer. He fell asleep hoping Brandon would stay with him forever.

Riley didn't know how long after that it was that he came to. Consciousness felt different this time, like something he might be able to keep instead of it slipping through his fingers.

Each sense seemed to come online separately. Sound first—monitors beeping, the low murmur of a television, Brandon snoring. Then the smell of antiseptic and a scent that was uniquely Brandon. Taste wasn't pleasant—his mouth was dry, and he really needed a mint. A warm hand held his, and his other palm lay on cool sheets.

When he opened his eyes, he found Brandon leaning on his folded arms on Riley's bed, dozing. He thought it was the best thing he had ever seen.

Riley must have twitched because Brandon jerked awake and sat up, staring at Riley like he had seen a miracle.

"You're awake!" Brandon reached for the call button. "He's awake!"

A nurse and doctor hurried into the room. Brandon stepped back, letting them check Riley, maintaining eye contact as much as he could.

"We need to do some tests, so we are going to ask you to step out, but we'll let you back in just as soon as we can," the nurse assured Brandon, ushering him to the door.

"Stay." Riley's hoarse voice made them all turn. "He stays." He held out his hand to Brandon, who took it and gave a squeeze, then stepped as far out of the way as he could so the team could check Riley over.

When they finished, the doctor looked to Riley, who anticipated her question.

"Brandon is my mate. You can speak in front of him. Please don't make him go."

The doctor nodded her acceptance. "All right. By the way, I'm Dr. Swanson. Your concussion is healing, but it's not going to be completely healed for a while, even though we're thrilled that you're awake. I'll schedule some tests tomorrow to see how much impact— short term and long term—we can expect. And I'll send you home with a list of side effects to watch for. I'm hoping, given your age and the nature of the injury, that healing will go well."

"So I have to stay?"

Dr. Swanson smiled. "There's really nowhere to go for now. We're all stuck at the hospital, given the storm, until the roads are cleared, and that won't be until at least tomorrow. Might as well make the best of it."

"What about everything else?" Riley asked.

"You've got some very mild frostbite, nothing that won't heal with a little TLC. Sounds like you were smart to bundle up and keep out of the wind," the doctor told him. "Your hypothermia hadn't reached the severe level, but it was very close. We've checked for organ damage and didn't find any signs. Pneumonia is a concern, so we'll watch for symptoms but haven't seen any yet. Otherwise, you shouldn't have any lasting effects. You must have a guardian angel watching out for you."

"More like a guardian moose." Riley looked at Brandon.

After Dr. Swanson and the nurse left, Brandon moved back to his bedside chair and took Riley's hand again. "Damn, it's good to see your eyes."

"Good to see you too. I really didn't think I would, there for a while."

Brandon leaned in and kissed him, slow and gentle. "Glad you're back." He sat in the chair, still holding hands. "I know we haven't been together long, but…you didn't tell me about your stalker ex."

"You didn't tell me you were a moose."

"Fair enough," Brandon acknowledged.

Riley sighed. "I really hoped that Tate would give up when I moved so far away. I realize now that he didn't love me, but I guess he couldn't stand admitting that he couldn't control me. And maybe I was a tasty, convenient meal."

"Meal?"

"He was a psi-vamp who could drain energy. That's how he trapped me—he drained a lot more than ever before, and I couldn't fight back," Riley replied. "I wanted to make a fresh start here and not bring all that baggage with me. And then I met you, and I didn't want my past to stain our relationship."

"If you weren't a nil, I probably would have read enough of your thoughts to suspect," Brandon said. "But I'm betting that because you're immune, his mojo didn't work as well on you—which might have saved your life."

"That's Dr. Jeffries's theory," Riley said. "If so, I'll never have been so happy to be unreadable."

"You aren't completely unreadable." Brandon stroked the back of Riley's hand as they talked. "I couldn't pick up words, but I felt when you got hit, and I knew you were scared and hurt. Maybe I'll only be able to read your emotions in an emergency, or maybe it will shift the longer we're together after the bite, but it's nice to know you're not totally closed to me."

"I'm glad. I like that." Riley stifled a yawn. "I'm tired. Who knew getting kidnapped was so exhausting?" He managed a wan smile and lifted a hand to touch Brandon's hair.

"Your moose is very handsome."

"Don't let him hear you—he'll get a swelled head," Brandon teased.

"Impressive antlers."

"Well hung?"

Riley groaned. "I can't believe you went there—although that's true too," he added with a sly grin. "Why didn't you tell me?"

Brandon sighed. "I wasn't quite sure how to bring it up. You accepted psychics, but people turning into animals is a lot to believe in."

"Dr. Jeffries gave me 'the talk.' He didn't out you—or anyone else —but he told me that shifters were real and that quite a bit of the town had a fuzzy side."

"Are you okay with it? My moose and I are a package deal." Brandon sounded hesitant.

Riley squeezed his hand and lifted it to kiss his knuckles. "Of course I am. And tell him thanks for saving me."

"He likes you. He knew as soon as he smelled you that you were our mate."

"When I was in the snow cave and didn't think I'd make it, I imagined us being together," Riley confessed. "All the way from now to being old farts in rocking chairs on the porch. And now that I'm not dying, I'd really like to make that happen."

"Move in with me," Brandon offered. "For one thing, I can make sure your head injury doesn't cause problems. But mostly, I just want you close—and in my bed."

"I'd like that," Riley said and felt a little shy. "But is it too quick? Are you sure?"

"I'm sure. My moose is sure. You're our mate. And as soon as you're cleared to leave here, if you're willing, I'd like to seal the deal and share a mating bite."

Riley's hand went to the hickey on his neck. "Will we be more connected?"

"I don't know for sure how much it will change things since you're a nil, but I think we'll sense more feelings, even if not words. That would be nice," Brandon admitted.

Riley yawned again. "I want to hear all about it—and someday, I want to see you shift. But I think I'm crashing."

"Rest. I'm going to grab a bite to eat, and I'll be right back," Brandon said. "I won't be gone long."

Riley closed his eyes when Brandon left, lightly dozing. He opened them again with a sigh when he heard footsteps and knew, even without looking, that the visitor wasn't Brandon.

Sheriff Arnell cleared his throat. "Sorry to bother you, but I need to ask a few questions. I'll keep it short."

Arnell was a tall, solidly built man with broad shoulders and a thick head of brown hair. With his newfound knowledge, Riley immediately thought, *bear shifter*, and wondered if he was right.

"That's okay," Riley told the nurse, who had looked to him for permission. "Might be a little scrambled, but I'll tell you what I can."

"How well did you know your attacker?" Arnell asked. "Tate Carson? Is that his name?"

"Tate was my ex-boyfriend. We'd been dating for about a year. I broke things off several months before I moved to Fox Hollow. He stalked me after we broke up. I came up with an exit plan—which is how I ended up here."

"Exit plan?" Arnell's head came up sharply. "Was he abusive before the breakup?"

"Not at first. But later, yeah. I'm almost positive he was a psi-vamp who fed on me without permission."

He braced himself for some sort of "didn't you know he was trouble" comment and relaxed a fraction when Arnell just nodded and made note of his reply.

"Were you aware of his background?"

Riley frowned. It hurt to think too hard, but Arnell's question didn't make sense. "Background? He never mentioned anything. It didn't come up."

"He had priors for assault and stalking. I ran a background check when you filed the restraining order with our office. You weren't the first to take one out against him," the sheriff replied. "Can you tell me what happened? Then I'll let you rest."

Riley recounted Tate confronting him in the parking lot, their argument, the way he felt drained, and being hit with the butt of Tate's gun. He told Arnell how they had argued over how fast Tate was driving and the skid that sent them over the hill.

"He hit you with his *unregistered, unlicensed* gun," the sheriff muttered. "I'm waiting on a ballistics report to see if it matches any weapons used in crimes. It was acquired illegally."

How could I have been so easy to fool?

Arnell seemed to guess his thoughts. "Guys like Tate are master manipulators. They don't show their scummy side until they think they have you hooked. You were smart to get out. I'm sorry that things got complicated."

"Thanks. What happens now?" Riley struggled with a tangle of emotions, none of which he felt ready to confront right now.

Arnel sighed. "Paperwork. Lots and lots of it. I've ordered an autopsy, although the cause of death seems clear. That'll tell us if he was under the influence of drugs. Still running a check on his truck to see if it was involved in anything illegal. Eventually, we'll contact next of kin to return the body."

"He never talked about family," Riley said. "I don't know whether he had any or not."

"Not your problem." The sheriff shrugged. "Now, I think you'd better rest. Thanks for your cooperation. I'm sure this is difficult."

"I wanted him to leave me alone, and I never wanted to see him again. But I didn't wish him dead."

Arnell met his eyes. "I've dealt with guys like him before. He wasn't going to go away on his own. It was always going to come down to him or you."

Riley shivered as the realization hit hard. "Thanks."

"Take care of yourself. I don't think I'll need anything more from you, but if I do, I know where to find you." The sheriff let himself out.

Riley struggled to remember the early days with Tate before things went bad. They met at a club. Tate was lively and outgoing, and they bonded over music. Later, Tate resented the time Riley spent with his guitar and the gigs he played. They fought. Riley refused to give up playing. Tate retaliated. Eventually, Riley walked out when it got to be too much. He always felt tired back then. Now, he realized Tate had been draining him.

If he had believed I would actually leave, he could have stopped me by making me too exhausted to do it. I'm lucky I got away.

Brandon came in as the sheriff left. "Everything okay?"

Riley sighed. "Just found out more about Tate I didn't know. God, I was an idiot."

Brandon moved to sit next to his bed and took his hand. "You're not an idiot. A bad person intentionally lied to you. That's not your fault."

He nodded. "I know—in my head. It's going to take a bit for the rest of me to catch up." Riley sniffed back tears. "Another good thing about the whole fated mates thing. It's meant to be."

"Yes, mates recognize each other. But we can take this at whatever pace you need," Brandon told him. "Fast or slow, we'll get to the same point. We belong together."

Riley squeezed his hand. "I refuse to let Tate have anything to do with us. I'm not going to give him that power. You're the best thing that ever happened to me. I want what we have. I'm not going to let the past get in the way."

Brandon leaned in and kissed him slowly and gently. "My moose and I are very proud of you."

Two days later, the storm had passed, and the roads were clear. Brandon pushed Riley in a wheelchair to the hospital's covered entrance and helped him into Brandon's Suburban.

"I already picked your Pilot up from the parking lot," Brandon told him. "Madden and I got your hotel room packed up and spoke to Steve. Your SUV and your stuff are at my place. You can figure out where you want everything to go when you feel up to it."

"I sold off everything that wouldn't fit in the Pilot when I left Jamestown. So I travel light."

Brandon squeezed his hand. "Then you've got a clean slate to make a fresh start. We'll fill in the blanks—together."

Once they reached the cabin, Brandon hesitated in the kitchen. "I already brought your stuff inside, but I figured you'd want to unpack it yourself." He paused. "Also, about where to put your clothing—I didn't want to assume that we're sharing a room. What do you want to do?" Brandon looked nervous.

"It's okay with me—is there an issue?" Riley had figured they would be sleeping together and now wondered if he had gotten ahead of them.

"No problem, none at all. I just…I'm not good at this." Brandon gave a deep sigh. "I don't want to screw anything up."

Riley reached out and brought Brandon into his arms. "Asking questions and being clear isn't going to do any harm. You can ask me anything."

"Me too. My moose was hoping we'd sleep in the same room. And so was I."

Now that Brandon was being open about his shifter side, Riley had to get used to him referring to his "other half" as having opinions of its own.

"How do you want me to unpack?" Riley stood with his hands on his hips, surveying the small cabin. "Where can I put my stuff? There isn't a lot."

"I already cleared half of the closet and dresser in the bedroom. And there are storage boxes under the bed for seasonal or bulky stuff," Brandon said.

"That should be fine. Otherwise, I have some knickknacks, books, my computer, and e-reader and chargers, that sort of thing. I left everything that I could live without just to leave Jamestown fast," Riley confessed.

This time, Brandon initiated the hug. "Most of my stuff is still from college or the furniture that came with the cabin. It could use an upgrade. We'll get what we need for a household together."

"I like the sound of that." Riley buried his face in Brandon's shoulder and breathed deep. He didn't have a shifter side, but something deep inside recognized "mate."

"Why don't you get your stuff put away, and I'll work on dinner." Brandon kissed Riley again. "If we keep this up, we'll end up in bed. You won't get unpacked, we won't eat dinner, and we'll die from starvation."

"Can't let that happen." Riley was happy despite still feeling the effects of his ordeal.

It didn't take long to figure out how to store his clothing in the drawers and part of the closet Brandon had cleared. Riley appreciated that Brandon had made more room than he needed, a generous move that made Riley feel welcome and wanted.

He plugged in his electronics and put the few knickknacks on top of the dresser until he could figure out a better location. They were small reminders of past vacations and trips to theme parks, happy times that didn't include Tate.

I don't know how he fooled me or what I ever saw in him. But back at the beginning, I cared.

Riley knew now that no attraction he had felt to anyone matched the mate bond with Brandon. *And we haven't even completed it. Maybe that's why things never worked out with anyone else. They weren't my mate.*

Riley put his guitar and keyboard in a corner of the living room. His amps and electronics were safely stowed at the hotel for when his gigs resumed after taking a few weeks off to recuperate. Dr. Jeffries had been very understanding and given him extensions on his class-work, putting the research project on hold until Riley was fully recovered.

The cabin was warm and cozy, and the mix of art, books, and tchotchkes from different games and fandoms was so thoroughly Brandon. He inhaled, taking in both the smell of dinner cooking and a scent that was very Brandon. *Home. Mate.*

Riley had been in survival mode since the crash and then focused on recovering so he could leave the hospital. There hadn't been time to process Tate's death, even though he had seen the body first-hand.

Now that the shock of the wreck had faded, Riley found himself thinking about Tate as if he were a stranger, a distancing reaction that he admitted to himself was probably a survival mechanism. Every-thing about Tate turned out to be a lie. Any fondness or attraction Riley had ever felt for him was long gone. He hadn't wished death on Tate, only to be left alone. But now, Riley felt detached, feeling only relief and the vague sadness he might feel for a total stranger.

Should I be guilty about not feeling more? At one time, I thought I cared for him. It's complicated enough I imagine I'll be talking to a therapist about it someday, but not right now.

I've started something good, and I'm not going to let Tate tarnish my rela-tionship with Brandon from beyond the grave.

"Dinner's ready," Brandon called, far sooner than Riley expected, and he realized he had been lost in his thoughts.

"You should have let me help." Riley joined Brandon in the kitchen.

"There wasn't much to do, and the sooner you get settled in here, the sooner we start our new future as a mated pair." Brandon leaned in for a kiss as he put the lasagna on the table. "Our first meal since you've moved in." Brandon gave Riley a warm smile that turned Riley's heart gooey.

"I never knew moose could cook," Riley teased.

"My moose doesn't." Brandon dug in. "He's more of a twigs and leaves kinda guy. If you're into that."

"Pass. I like this much better." Riley took a bite and closed his eyes, savoring. "This is really good."

"Well, at least you won't starve to death." Brandon chuckled. "I like taking care of you."

"I want to take good care of you too." That was new for Riley. His prior relationships, even the more successful ones, had never moved beyond the polite supportiveness of friends with benefits. Now that he knew the difference, he couldn't believe the lack hadn't seemed glaring.

When they finished in the kitchen, Riley was still feeling good despite being more tired than usual. His headache had eased, and his libido resurfaced.

"I've missed you." Riley snuggled close to Brandon on the couch after they cleaned the kitchen and put in a movie. "Let me show you how much."

The wide couch let them lie facing each other. Riley pulled Brandon into a kiss, starting slow and gradually growing more heated. He licked at Brandon's lips, seeking entry, and then deepened their connection with his tongue, tasting and savoring his partner.

"I can't get enough of you." He was surprised at the huskiness of his voice.

"You taste as good as you smell." Brandon let his hands roam over Riley's body, exploring and laying claim. Riley loved being able to touch Brandon all over, from his broad shoulders to his solid chest, where he lavished attention on the dusky nipples with his fingers and tongue.

Riley slipped a hand between Brandon's legs and smiled at how hard his partner was already. "You like this?" He thought Brandon's body already made the answer clear. His own cock was straining against his jeans, seeking release.

"Uh-huh." Brandon returned the favor and stroked Riley through the denim. He worked Riley's belt open and unzipped his pants, reaching inside and freeing his cock from his boxer briefs.

Riley caught his breath at the friction of Brandon's palm against the sensitive skin, only partly eased by pre-come. He hurried to return the favor, and they lay together, stroking each other with increasing urgency. Brandon reached into the space between the couch cushions and took out a tube of lube stashed from their last make-out session.

"I wasn't a Boy Scout, but I believe in being prepared." Brandon squirted some onto his palm before resuming his touch, faster now, propelling Riley toward the finish line.

Riley did the same, jerking them both at the same pace, pressing kisses against Brandon's chest as their pleasure built.

He felt his release rising from heat deep in his groin, balls drawing up, and knew he wouldn't last much longer. Riley pushed close to Brandon, angling his neck, and bared his throat for the mating bite.

"Please." Riley teetered on the edge of orgasm.

Brandon licked and sucked at the sensitive skin, working Riley with a firm grip. When Riley came, Brandon's lips were on the hickey, warm and claiming.

Riley tensed for the pain of a bite as his climax washed over him. He came hard, encircled by Brandon's arm, surrounded by his scent, Brandon's mouth on his neck. Seconds later, he felt Brandon come as well.

Only when the haze of his orgasm faded did Riley realize Brandon's teeth had never broken his skin.

He drew back to meet Brandon's eyes, confused and hurt. "Why?"

Brandon kissed him tenderly. "The bite is supposed to happen during penetrative sex. It's part of the claiming. And you don't have medical permission for that kind of strenuous activity."

"I need a doctor's note before you'll fuck me?" Riley couldn't help feeling disappointed and a little outraged.

"Yep. I discussed it with Dr. Swanson. It might be an abundance of caution, but if you black out and fall off the bed, you could make the concussion worse." Brandon sounded entirely too logical.

"I've never fallen off a bed during sex in my life." Riley felt vaguely insulted.

Brandon kissed him, seeking forgiveness with big brown eyes. "I don't want to hold back when we fuck for the first time. I don't want either of us to worry or think about anything except chasing pleasure.

"Maybe we'll do it slow, or maybe we'll go rough and ready—or a little of both. There's so much I want to explore with you. But if I'm worried about hurting you or you're uncomfortable, it's going to spoil the moment. And I want us to remember your claiming for the rest of our lives."

Brandon stripped out of his T-shirt and wiped them both off, a gesture Riley took as conciliatory. "Believe me, I want to be in you so bad, want to know how you feel. Want to complete our bond and see where it takes us. But I can't enjoy it if I'm worried that I'll set back your progress, and if I hurt you because we got too enthusiastic, I'd have a hard time forgiving myself."

Riley appreciated Brandon's concern and recognized that his partner's self-control was a form of love. But his cock didn't understand, and Riley's disappointment over having to wait made it hard to be patient.

"How soon? I want to be everything to you."

Brandon kissed him again, tender and hungry. "Soon. You go back to the doctor in a week. If everything's looking good, she thought we'd be fine by then."

"Cockblocked by a concussion," Riley sighed.

"Don't be angry, babe. Once we start, we can stay in bed for days if you want. Believe me, holding back isn't fun for me either. But it'll be better in the long run. And I love you, so I've gotta take care of you."

Brandon's low voice and gentle touch broke through Riley's pique. "All right," Riley reluctantly agreed. "But I'm gonna hold you to the bit about staying in bed for days."

11

BRANDON

Brandon kissed him again. "I've got an idea. Wanna see my moose?"

Riley laughed. "From anyone else, I'd think that was a euphemism. Of course I do."

"All right. Get your coat."

Riley gave him a quizzical look. "Does it hurt to shift? I don't want you to be uncomfortable just to show me. I'm sure I'll see at some point."

Brandon shook his head. "Shifting doesn't hurt unless I push it too fast, which isn't healthy for other reasons. It's like doing a really good stretch, the kind that makes you feel like you've worked out all your knots. And then I'm a moose. On the other side, it's like curling into myself, only I keep curling and curling and then, poof! No more moose."

Riley looked at him quizzically. "Where does all the mooseness go? You're a big guy, but you're a huge moose. The antlers alone are gigantic. I don't understand how all that fits in here." He rested his hand on Brandon's chest.

"That's the nice thing about being a born shifter—I don't have to understand how it works. I just think about it and it happens."

"Some shifters aren't born that way?"

"We avoid using the 'were' prefix because it's got a lot of stigma attached to it," Brandon replied. "Some were-creatures are born that way. Most turn because of a bite—which is fine, as long as it's consensual. They know what it was like to be purely human, so I've heard that learning to shift is harder for them. I think everyone gets the hang of it eventually."

"The world is a much more complicated place than I ever knew," Riley replied.

"Come on," Brandon said. "I want you to see my moose. He's been bugging me to show him off. And then you can help warm me up."

Riley grabbed his coat and followed Brandon out the back door. "That's my changing area." Brandon pointed at his shelter. "Keeps me out of the wind. Avoids freezing the dangly bits."

"I'm fond of those bits," Riley pointed out. "Gotta keep them safe."

"Give me a minute once I 'moose out,' and then you can pet me if you want to. The antlers are very sensitive. Touching them is like stroking my arm."

"I think I have a new fetish," Riley replied.

"Kinky."

Brandon went to the changing area and stripped down quickly, glad for the windbreak but still shivering. The change came fast, transforming muscle and sinew. He had watched others shift, but Brandon realized he had never shifted in front of someone. Once he could talk again, he would have to ask what it looked like.

It looks majestic. He's finally getting to see us in all our moosely glory. He was barely conscious the last time.

I don't think "moosely" is a word.

It should be. It describes our "mooseness."

Also not a word.

His moose made a noise like blowing raspberries but much louder and slurpier.

Brandon stepped out of the windbreak, feeling unexpectedly self-conscious, as if he were being seen naked for the first time instead of transforming into a massive forest creature.

Riley's eyes were wide, and he stared at Brandon in wonder. "Wow. You're beautiful. Handsome. Magnificent."

Brandon ducked his head in acknowledgment. Even in moose form, their not-yet-complete mate bond still provided impressions of Riley's emotions, which echoed his spoken praise.

He likes us. He thinks we look good. Brandon's moose preened, and he realized that his other half had been afraid Riley might not approve.

Of course he does. We do.

Riley moved forward hesitantly as if Brandon might spook in his new form. Brandon waited patiently, head down so Riley could pet his neck and antlers.

"You are so…just, wow." Riley stroked Brandon's slick, short hair. He scratched behind one of Brandon's ears, which tickled, making him twitch.

"I think I have an antler fetish." Riley played his fingers lightly across the velvety surface.

No one had ever touched Brandon's antlers before, and he shivered, surprised at just how sensitive they were.

"So soft," Riley whispered. "And big. Your antlers are almost wider across than I am tall. That's…impressive." He paused. "Moose shed their antlers, right?"

Brandon nodded.

"Does it hurt?"

Brandon shook his head and made the closest noise to a chuckle he could manage. Riley stroked a finger down the bridge of Brandon's nose, looking into his dark eyes.

Brandon snuffled into Riley's palm.

"Oooh. Moose snot," Riley laughed, wiping his hands on his pants. He stepped closer and put his arms around Brandon's neck.

"Thank you for saving me. I love you—and your moose." Riley buried his face in Brandon's fur.

They stood together for a few moments, and then Riley moved back. "Do you need to go frolic a little since you're shifted?"

Brandon gave him the side-eye at that and then nodded.

"Run free, sweet moose." Riley gave a big grin and a slap to his hindquarters then watched as Brandon loped off toward the tree line, before he headed back inside.

He has good taste in moose.

I think we're the only one he's ever seen for real.

Still, his moose replied. *I approve.*

That's good because I'm keeping him.

Since he had gone to the trouble of shifting, Brandon took time to nibble at the twigs, bark, and needles his moose preferred. It felt good to stretch his legs in this form, and he walked a mile or so before returning to the cabin, not wanting to leave Riley alone for long.

Changing back left him shivery, and he hurried into the house. "Miss me?" Brandon peeled off his coat and slipped out of his boots.

"Of course," Riley called from the kitchen, where he had a pan of hot chocolate on the stove. "Drink this—and then I'll be glad to warm up any dangly bits that are still cold."

"There's a lot to be said for having fur down there." Brandon sat at the table and accepted the hot mug from Riley. "None of the equipment gets cold in moose form."

"No moose-scaping?"

Brandon rolled his eyes. "That would defeat the purpose. But I've got no problem trimming the hedges in human form."

Riley gave him a dirty grin. "It's nice not to get hair stuck in my teeth."

"If manscaping means more blow jobs, sign me up."

"Once you finish your hot chocolate, I've got other ways to get you warm." Riley came up behind Brandon and leaned in close. "Gotta check very closely for frostbite."

Riley went down to his knees between Brandon's legs, mouthing at his bulge through the denim and running his fingers up his sensitive inner thighs. Brandon set his drink aside since being doused by hot chocolate would only be sexy if Riley then licked it off.

Hold that thought for the future.

Riley teased Brandon until his hard cock strained at the zipper, and Brandon groaned, spreading his legs wider to give his swollen member some space.

"Please, Riley," he groaned. "Make me feel good."

Riley grinned and made a show of unbuckling Brandon's belt. He made Brandon wait, moving the zipper one tooth at a time, as his left hand slid beneath Brandon to massage his balls and taint.

"So good. Want you."

Riley opened Brandon's fly, and Brandon lifted enough for him to slide his jeans down, leaving him in his briefs.

"Already leaking for me. So sexy," Riley said in a rough voice that sounded like all Brandon's dirty dreams.

Riley mouthed his bulge through the cotton, exhaling hot air against the swollen dick and rolling Brandon's balls with his other hand.

He slid Brandon's underwear down, and his cock sprang free. "So big—and all for me."

"All yours. Come on. Wanna feel you suck me."

"Tell me what it's going to be like when we finally fuck." Riley licked at the crown and teased his tongue up and down the shaft. "Talk dirty to me."

"Gonna lick you all over," Brandon breathed. "Mark you up so everyone knows you're mine. Drive you wild, teasing your nipples."

"Yeah?"

"Find your sensitive spots where I can make you crazy and see if I can make you come just like that," Brandon continued as if he hadn't heard Riley. "I want to suck your cock and your balls and lick your taint. Want to rim you until you scream."

Riley had to press the heel of his hand against his own aching hard-on until he wasn't in imminent danger of blowing his load.

"Go on," he said in a strangled voice before returning to his task with renewed vigor. He sucked in his cheeks and hummed, then went back to licking Brandon like a popsicle. Brandon squirmed, and Riley doubled down, alternating humming and sucking as he rolled Brandon's balls in his fingers.

"Take my time opening you up with my fingers and my tongue," Brandon went on, breathless. "Get you sloppy wet and loose so you can take me. Finger your magic spot and make you come so you're nice and relaxed. Can't decide if I want to fuck you from behind or have you ride my cock on my lap. Bend you over the table. Pick you up and fuck you against the wall."

Riley got his fingers nice and wet and then slipped them along Brandon's taint. He eased one finger into Brandon's tight pucker, rewarded by Brandon's sharp intake of breath. Riley kept up his rhythm with his mouth as he curled his finger to hit Brandon's sweet spot.

Brandon arched and cried out, coming down Riley's throat and leaking out of the corners of his mouth. Riley swallowed and licked his lips. Brandon leaned forward with his elbows on Riley's shoulders and panted. Riley gave one more lick to Brandon's over-sensitive cock to make him shiver.

12

RILEY

"Stand up," Brandon said, voice wrecked.

Riley obeyed, knowing Brandon could see just how aroused he was by what they had done.

"Take off your jeans. Give me a show."

That command sent a frisson of desire through Riley that nearly ended things before they got started.

He let his hips sway as he slowly unbuckled his belt and tossed it aside. He had never stripped for anyone before, but he'd seen a lot of videos and gone to a couple of clubs in Rochester.

Riley danced to the music in his mind, humming softly. He toed his socks off and pushed his jeans down, letting them fall to the floor before kicking them aside. Then he turned around, shaking his ass, doing some deep squats, and pushing up, ass-first, right in front of Brandon.

He wants a show? I can do that.

Riley turned back to face Brandon and let his hands run over his chest. He stopped to tease his nipples, still swaying his hips in a private dance. He kept his left hand busy with his nipples while the right slid down and stroked his cock through his briefs.

"Take them off and touch yourself."

Riley discovered that this new assertive side of Brandon turned him on. He expected them to switch once they could finally do anal, and he liked to trade off roles, but Riley was finding out he liked a bossy moose.

His breath caught as he slid his briefs over his throbbing cock. *If I can't last and lose it all over him, will he be turned on or mad? Might not have a choice about it—so damn close.*

He realized that his worry was another unwelcome leftover from Tate and did his best to push those thoughts from his mind.

Riley kicked his underwear aside. He wrapped his fingers around his cock and slowly stroked from base to tip, taking his time because he could feel his climax building.

"So goddamn sexy," Brandon growled. He slid off his chair to kneel in front of Riley and batted his hands out of his way.

Brandon's big hands palmed Riley's ass, each one claiming a globe with a squeeze as he pulled him closer. He went down on Riley in one move, taking him all the way to the root and constricting his throat.

That did it. Riley shouted Brandon's name as he came, his release pulsing down Brandon's throat. He wasn't sure he could have remained standing if Brandon's grip on his ass hadn't kept him upright. At the height of his climax, Brandon palmed his cheeks apart and slid a finger down his crack and into his hole.

His orgasm seemed to come in waves and last forever. Finally spent, Riley's knees buckled. Brandon caught him as he fell, going to the floor with him cradled against Brandon's muscled chest.

It took Riley a couple of minutes to form words. That left him in a floaty place of sensation, and he became aware of feelings washing over him. *Love. Protection. Fondness. Lust. Loyalty.*

He didn't hear words, but the emotions came through loud and clear. He tried to think the same things back at Brandon, unsure what it would take to ease the mental silence between them.

"Shh. I hear you." Brandon pushed a sweaty lock of hair out of Riley's eyes. "I feel what you're sending. And it's enough." He leaned in to kiss Riley, letting him taste himself on Brandon's lips.

"When you bite me, is it going to be even more intense?" The world narrowed to just the two of them lying tangled together on the cabin floor.

"That's what they say," Brandon replied in a throaty whisper.

"I might not survive," Riley chuckled, "but what a way to go."

A WEEK LATER, Riley went for his check-up.

"Cleared for active duty," he told Brandon from his phone when he left the hospital. "We can make up for lost time."

Riley walked into the kitchen and saw a red heart-shaped helium balloon floating above the table, which held a bouquet of roses and a cake made out of a Twinkie and two strategically-placed cupcakes at one end to look like a cock and balls.

"Happy Fuckability Day!" Brandon tossed a handful of penis-shaped confetti in the air. Then Riley realized Brandon wore nothing but an apron.

He started laughing, touched by the gesture and, at the same time, aware of how totally bonkers it all was. "This is…amazing. I feel very desired."

"You're wearing way too many clothes," Brandon growled. "Let's take this party to the bedroom. Here. Let me help."

Brandon took Riley in his arms and kissed him until Riley was panting for air. The thin apron did nothing to hide Brandon's erection, and by then, Riley was sporting a boner too.

"Don't need this." Brandon lifted the hem of Riley's shirt and tugged it over his head. He kissed his way down Riley's neck, stopping to lightly nip and lick at the hickey before running his hands along Riley's sides, down his chest, over his taut nipples, and down his back.

"Still too many clothes." Brandon held Riley close with his left arm while he undid his belt with his right hand and pushed jeans and underwear down far enough that Riley could step out of them as he toed off his socks.

"Much better."

Riley loosened the tie of Brandon's apron and slipped it over his head. "Now we're even."

Brandon walked Riley backward into the bedroom as they continued to kiss and fondle. They fell onto the bed, intertwined, barely pausing long enough to breathe.

"I don't want long and slow this time," Riley panted as Brandon slipped a hand between his legs, stroking his cock. "I want you."

"Need to make it good for you. I've got to get you ready."

Riley gave him a smug grin. "Are you sure about that?"

Brandon slipped a finger along Riley's taint to his hole and found it slick with lube and filled with a sizable butt plug.

"I'm impressed." He barely hid a chuckle. "Guess I don't need to ask if you're sure."

"More mating, less talking. Fuck me and bite me. Let's get with the program."

Riley slipped off to the bathroom to remove the butt plug, and while he was gone, Brandon pulled back the covers, slipping into bed to await his return. Riley paused in the doorway to take in the view. Naked Brandon made a very pretty picture, especially with his cock standing at attention.

He crossed to the bed and prowled toward Brandon on his hands and knees, crossing the mattress until he straddled his partner, letting Brandon's thick cock slide up and down between his butt cheeks. Then he raised himself up, guided the tip of Brandon's dick to the entry of his hole, and eased the head into his ready entrance.

Brandon's hand gripped his hips, steadying him. Riley let his head fall back with the intensity of the burn as his body made room for Brandon's sizable dick.

"Take it slow. We've got all night," Brandon cautioned in a voice like whiskey and sin.

It had been a while for Riley, which prompted the inspiration for the butt plug. He tried to relax as Brandon eased inside inch by inch.

Brandon encouraged him by swirling his tongue around Riley's sensitive nipples, then licked a stripe up the center of his chest and began to mouth at his neck.

"You're doing so good for me," Brandon murmured. "So tight. Feel awesome."

Impatient, Riley pushed down until Brandon was completely seated, balls deep, and they both groaned in pleasure.

"Move," Brandon growled.

Riley lifted himself up and then down, slowly at first, then faster, setting up a rhythm. Brandon reached between them, perking up Riley's cock, which had softened with the initial burn until he was also hard and dripping.

Brandon kissed Riley, wet and open-mouthed, and sucked on his tongue while slowly working his cock. Riley didn't expect this time to be lingering and drawn out. There would be plenty of time for that. Now, he had mating on his mind.

"You sure?" Brandon blew across the tender skin of the hickey.

"Yes. Do it."

Riley arched in Brandon's arms as teeth broke skin, painful yet erotic. Without needing to think about it, he bent forward and did the same, biting into the meat at the juncture of Brandon's neck and shoulder, deep enough to draw blood and leave a scar.

A frisson of energy sizzled through Riley like completing a circuit. His orgasm surged at the same moment, carrying him away with pleasure, and Brandon thrust faster and harder, indicating his own rising climax.

Riley thought he might have whited out for a few seconds, and it took a moment to regain his senses, making him feel drunk with pleasure. He felt sated, but more than that, Riley felt a warm cocoon of love and protectiveness that came from inside his mind, not an outside observation.

Brandon?

Brandon nuzzled at Riley's throat, licking over the fresh bite, kissing away the sting.

Riley didn't hear words, but he felt a wash of emotions—happiness, satisfaction, pride, dedication. He wasn't sure if this was the mating bond, but he did his best to send back his own feelings, validating and confirming.

"Can you feel what I'm thinking?" Riley whispered, like sharing a secret between them.

"Uh-huh. Can you?"

"I think so. It's…nice."

Brandon eased them down on their sides and gently slipped out. He reached for tissues from the bedside box and cleaned them up, then rolled onto his back with Riley beside him, his head cradled on Brandon's shoulder. Just to be safe, he brought out two square bandages and some antibiotic salve for them to patch the bites.

"Will we be able to sense each other's thoughts all the time, or just after sex or near-death experiences?" Riley asked.

"I'm not sure. Guess we'll have to find out. It could change over time, get stronger, and happen more often. Are you okay with that?"

"Uh-huh," Riley murmured. "Definitely makes it harder to have a fight. Which is a good thing. Does a mate bond do anything else?"

"Depends on who you talk to," Brandon replied. "It might also differ among types of shifters. We're only now just 'growing our own' experts to study our biology in a safe way. Some say it brings the two partners' life forces into sync. Lore says that fated mates don't survive losing each other."

"Tragically romantic. Anything else?"

Brandon turned to face Riley. "I honestly never studied the lore because until I met you, I didn't think I'd ever find a fated mate. Then I saw you and knew for sure."

"Smelled me is more like it." Riley leaned in to kiss Brandon on the nose. He realized there was still one piece missing.

"Can I watch you shift again? Not right now—you'd break the bed. But sometime? Is it too private?"

Brandon chuckled. "You might find it unnerving until you get used to seeing it, but shifting isn't private for the reasons you might think. There are times when most of Fox Hollow shifts and goes for a run in their fur. Shifters can't change in their clothes—or at least, the clothes don't change with them—so none of us are prudish about nudity. We just don't shift in front of outsiders because we don't want to be on the six o'clock news."

"Makes sense." Riley reached out and stroked Brandon's long hair. "Are you disappointed to have a mate who isn't a shifter?"

Brandon shook his head. "Are you kidding? I have *you*. And you've got your own gifts. I'm just glad that I found you and we're together. Nothing else matters."

Riley snuggled close to Brandon, content in the circle of his arms. He breathed in the scent of his sweat, their sex, and something that was completely Brandon. He might not be a telepath, but the emotions that washed over him warmed his heart and soothed his soul.

Loved. Cherished. Safe.

Riley did his very best to send those same feelings back to Brandon. He felt the burn of the fresh bite, knowing he had found his forever moose, and smiled, grateful to be *home*.

RILEY FELT a bit better every day that passed after the wreck. Follow-up visits cleared him on his concussion, while muscle aches gradually went away and bruises faded.

Nightmares kept their own schedule.

The first ones happened in the hospital right after he regained consciousness. Riley relived the terrifying moments in the car, arguing with Tate, skidding on the ice, and then going over the side of the slope and waking up in the wreckage.

Sometimes, the script rewrote itself. Tate fired the gun he had brandished in the parking lot, and Riley died on the spot. His mind replayed the wreck, versions where Tate wasn't dead and followed Riley from the car, confronting him in the bloody snow, or where Riley left Tate behind in the car, injured but screaming curses, and the pickup exploded in a fireball.

Other versions stuck to the facts until Riley reached the top of the hill, but ended when he fell asleep in his snow cave before Brandon could rescue him.

There were variations. Sometimes Tate kidnapped Brandon, forcing Riley into a frantic search and ended with him bargaining for Brandon's safety, usually by trading himself as a hostage. In a few versions, Riley and Tate struggled over the gun, and someone got shot.

This night, Riley woke, panting and drenched in sweat, heart thudding. In the dream, he and Tate had struggled for the gun, and it went off, killing Brandon, who died in his arms.

"Riley?" Brandon's sleep-rough voice murmured. "It's okay, babe. You're safe. I'm safe. It's over. No one's going to hurt you."

Riley bit back a sob, unable to let go of the smell of blood, the weight of Brandon's body in his arms, the way his eyes stared without seeing. "He...the gun...you—"

"Shh." Brandon sat up and enfolded Riley in his arms, pulling him against his chest and stroking his hair. "I'm here. He's never going to hurt anyone again. Just breathe."

Riley sniffled, burying his face against Brandon and squeezing him tight. He took in Brandon's scent and the heat of his body, trying to convince himself that this was real.

"I'm sorry," he murmured. "You're not getting any sleep because of me and my stupid bad dreams."

"Hey. Your dreams aren't stupid. And there's no one I'd rather be sleep-deprived with," Brandon replied gently, an attempt to lighten the mood that Riley appreciated. "The doctor said it was a normal response to trauma. It's going to take time."

Riley nodded, but the gap between knowing with his head and believing with his heart seemed vast. "And normal people could see a psychic therapist and be able to share what they were seeing and feeling, but my freakish 'immune' brain doesn't work right."

Brandon pushed him away just far enough for their eyes to meet. "You are perfectly normal. Your immune ability isn't 'freakish.' Everyone copes differently. Trauma takes time to process. That's what the therapist at the hospital told you. Just talking without the psychic stuff works for most people."

"Can you pick up what I'm feeling through the bond?" Riley hated how damaged and weak he felt.

"Yes. It wakes me. I don't get words, but I pick up more images and feelings than I did before the bite. And I try to send back calming, safe thoughts." Brandon combed his fingers through Riley's sweat-soaked hair and pressed kisses to his temple.

"I feel them—and I try to follow those thoughts out of the nightmare. Tate's dead. I wish he'd go away for good. I feel…haunted."

"Jeffries sent a medium to the crash site," Brandon reminded him. "There was no spirit present. Tate's been cremated, and the mediums did a banishing ceremony with the ashes. They're buried in blessed, warded ground with binding spells. The only ghosts are in your mind."

"It would be easier to get rid of them if they weren't," Riley sighed.

Gradually, Riley felt the tension seep out of his exhausted body, and he slumped against Brandon. "Thank you."

"That's what mates are for," Brandon said. "Do you want to try to go back to sleep, or should I make hot chocolate and put in one of our cartoon DVDs for a while?"

Riley felt selfish for asking, but he was afraid to try to fall asleep again just yet. "Hot chocolate and Bugs Bunny, please."

Brandon chuckled. "Coming right up. We can wrap up in a blanket and snuggle."

"What about you getting some sleep?"

"I'll be fine." Brandon shrugged. "Moose in the wild catnap for five minutes at a time."

"Don't you mean, 'moose-nap'?" Despite everything, Riley couldn't resist the humor.

Brandon kissed him. "Come on. You can make a comfy nest on the floor in front of the couch while I make the hot chocolate. I'll even let you pick which disc to watch."

The banked fire still warmed the living room. Riley watched the glowing embers for a few minutes, entranced and welcoming the diversion. Then he pulled pillows and throw blankets onto the floor to make a cozy pit in front of the television and chose a disc with several of his favorite episodes.

"Pillow therapy," as Brandon called it, worked even if Riley sometimes felt chagrinned at needing the comfort of childhood favorites as an adult. Brandon—and Dr. Jeffries—assured him there was no shame in reaching for the safety of predictable experiences to help heal, and

Riley didn't have the spoons to put up an argument he didn't really want to win.

Hot chocolate, soft pillows, warm snuggles, and familiar cartoon hijinks lulled Riley into dozing, safe in Brandon's arms at some point in the wee hours of the morning.

He was surprised to find how late they had slept when he finally roused without a bad dream. "Did I make you late for anything?"

Brandon shook his head. "Not today. I have some preparation to do for a snowshoe hike tomorrow, but there's nothing on the calendar for today. Stay where you are. I'll put in a new disk, and we can eat sugary cereal in front of the TV like we're kids again."

"I love you so much. My guardian moose."

"We take good care of our mate."

OVER THE NEXT WEEKS, the nightmares gradually subsided between talking with a therapist, guided hypnosis, and cuddling with his mate. They came less often, lasted for a shorter time, and no longer seemed terrifyingly real. "Thank you for putting up with me," Riley said one night after a less frequent bad dream.

"You're my mate. It's not 'putting up with,' it's 'taking care of,'" Brandon corrected in a gentle tone.

"You've helped a lot." Riley held Brandon's hand on the couch as they re-watched a favorite comedy movie. "I know we don't have the full mate-bond telepathy, but 'thinking at each other' really does seem to help."

"Good to know. Maybe over time that will get stronger, and maybe it won't, but however it ends up, it's our bond, and that's good enough," Brandon assured him.

"Jeffries and the psychics are interested in how completing our bond impacted my 'immunity,'" Riley told him. "So half the town knows we did the deed."

"Like anyone doubted." Brandon snorted. "But I imagine it would be a unique case for them—a human bonded to a shifter on top of your ability."

"More like my inability." Despite Jeffries's encouragement, Riley had difficulty thinking about his psychic shielding as a positive.

"Hey, don't trash talk my mate," Brandon replied, like he always did when the subject came up. "I'm glad Jeffries expanded the time-frame on the study to see if things change the longer we're mated."

"I'm not sure that whatever he learns is going to help a lot of people—I don't know that there are a bunch of nils out there."

Brandon shrugged. "Might be. They might not even realize they are. No gift evolves without a purpose. Even though I can sense more of your feelings through our mate bond, I still find the lack of psychic noise to be very calming."

"That's what all the psychics say at the Institute. I guess I could be the office mascot, like some places let you bring in a dog for stress relief."

"Wasn't what I was thinking, but sure, go for it." Brandon laughed.

Their new couch made a visual statement of starting a fresh life together. The sofa had a retro "overstuffed" look in a saddle blanket pattern, and it was as wide as a twin bed, so cuddling wasn't a problem. Riley decided that the next piece on his wish list was a double recliner.

Moving in with Brandon had been less of an adjustment than Riley expected, based on his memories of college dorms and apartment roommates. He and Brandon just seemed to fit, and while they sometimes debated the best location to store something, finding common ground wasn't difficult.

Is it all due to the mate bond? It seemed like a lot to attribute to one factor, but Riley couldn't dispute that living with someone else—even his family when he was growing up—had never been so smooth. *Maybe the bond plus compatible zodiac signs. We're both big on communication, showing affection, and touch. Whatever the reason, I'm all for it.*

———

Two months after the wreck, Riley and Brandon went cross-country skiing under a full moon. The wide-open park was mostly flat, with a few rolling hills. Riley didn't feel the cold. Skiing warmed him up, and

Brandon had gone over Riley's winter wardrobe and suggested upgrades that were better suited for Fox Hollow's weather and more durable than his old gear.

A fresh powder glistened in the moonlight, and the twigs and branches fairly twinkled from their coating of ice.

"It's sort of magical out here." Riley stared up at the open sky. Away from cities, he could see so many more stars.

"Definitely magical."

Something in Brandon's voice made Riley turn to see Brandon go down on one knee and hold out a small box, flipped open to show two matching gold rings.

"Are those—"

"Riley Henderson, my love and my mate, will you also do me the honor of being my husband?" Brandon asked.

Despite the cold, Riley nearly melted. "Yes! Oh, God. Yes!" Skis kept him from jumping up and down, and mittens muffled the sound when he clapped his hands, but Brandon's huge smile made it clear he understood.

"Good." Brandon rose and tucked the ring box into a zippered pocket. "Now let's go home before we freeze off our nuts."

"I've got plans for those nuts," Riley teased. "I like your moose knuckle too."

As they skied back in the moonlight, Riley tuned into his mate, doing his best to pick up on Brandon's emotions through their bond. *Happiness. Satisfaction. Contentment and…horniness.*

Well, we're on the same page. He tried to "beam" those same feelings back to Brandon, hoping Brandon could read at least that much.

That night, they made love in front of the fireplace on a soft pile of blankets. Riley loved the way the firelight gave Brandon's skin a golden glow and brought out the highlights in his chestnut hair.

Maybe it shouldn't have been a surprise that communicating through their bond felt strongest—barring dire circumstances—when they made love. Linking their bodies seemed to complete the circuit to link their minds, making the emotions shared through their connection even stronger.

"Have you thought about how you want it? The wedding?" Riley felt warm and sated in front of the fire.

"Figured we'd plan it together." Brandon twined their fingers.

"Sure, but you've been in town longer than I have. Have you seen anything that you filed away 'just in case'?"

Brandon laughed. "Honestly? Before you showed up, I wasn't sure I'd ever meet the right person. I avoided thinking about anything like that because it was too depressing."

Riley chuckled. "I'm sorry you felt like that, but I'm glad you were still available when I got here."

"How about you? I'm fairly open-minded, although running off to Florida for a Disney World wedding might be complicated," Brandon said, and Riley laughed out loud.

"I'm pretty sure there was a moose or two in some of those animated movies, or at least a reindeer."

"Not the same. Distant cousins," Brandon sniffed. "Moose have prettier antlers."

Riley raised his hands in surrender. "No argument from me about that. I'm the guy with the antler fetish, remember?"

"I'm just glad that transfers to my other 'prong.'"

Riley rolled his eyes. "Moose jokes." He sobered. "About the wedding? I really don't need anything fancy. Staying here in Fox Hollow with all our friends would be lovely. I'm even okay with doing it at the hotel. I've seen how they decorate, and they do up the ballroom real pretty. The food is good, and people don't have to worry as much about the weather."

"You play multiple gigs there a month. Are you sure that's special enough?"

Riley loved Brandon for asking. He leaned in and kissed him on the nose. "I'm marrying you. That's plenty special."

"How about the honeymoon? Do you have a dream vacation tucked away in your mind?"

Riley thought for a moment. "There are a lot of places I'd eventually like to see, but it doesn't have to be right now. If we want to save on plane fare, there's that super-fancy lodge up in Lake Placid that might be nice. Huge fireplaces, s'more cookouts, really cool décor, and people say the food is good."

"Are the beds comfy? Because no matter where we go, I plan to spend most of it under the covers with you," Brandon told him with a wicked wink.

"Now that you mention it, their site had extra kudos for how comfortable they were," Riley replied.

"Well then, move it to the top of the list. I've always wanted to check out that place too."

"I don't care as long as I'm with you." Riley snuggled closer. He could hear the wind outside, and occasionally a gust made sparks fly in the firebox. Despite the storm, Riley was toasty warm, even naked, between the fire on one side and Brandon on the other.

Even in his human form, Brandon definitely ran hot, preferring to sleep naked except on the coldest nights. Riley wasn't about to complain about the view, although he opted for sleep pants and a T-shirt unless he spent the night plastered against Brandon.

"It's a small town. Who do we invite? I don't want to hurt anyone's feelings," Riley said as the thought suddenly occurred to him. "Or do you want us to make our vows with just the two of us and then throw a big party?"

"It's not like I had online photo boards of wedding ideas," Brandon said in a wry tone. "I didn't think it was something I needed to worry about. But now that you mention it—maybe we just post an open notice. 'Wedding at this time, reception to follow. Everyone welcome.' That way no one feels left out."

"That would work if we did light appetizers and a cash bar," Riley mused. "We could have a DJ and a justice of the peace. Keep it simple."

"Is that okay? Did you have your heart set on something more formal?"

Riley chuckled. "Not disappointed at all. I never was much for church weddings. Outdoor ceremonies always seemed like tempting fate. And the hotel is pretty enough that people come from all over to get hitched there, so why make it complicated?"

"That's very practical. My moose is impressed." Brandon leaned in for a kiss.

"He can be our moose-of-honor or the 'best moose,'" Riley returned.

"He says he's always the best moose," Brandon relayed his internal dialogue. Riley had gotten used to Brandon's inner moose having opinions and making them known.

"He's sort of an invisible friend who really exists," Riley joked. "And he's a very good moose."

"He knows he is. Don't give him a swelled head."

Riley settled against Brandon, happy to be quiet and together. They would need to move to the bed since the fire would die down overnight, but right now, safe in Brandon's arms, there was nowhere he would rather be.

EPILOGUE
BRANDON

Three months later.

"Prepare to be in the presence of greatness." Drew weighed the bowling ball in both hands before stalking forward with a backswing and sending the ruby-red ball barreling down the lane.

His companions cat-called when all his mojo resulted in a split.

"Let the grown-ups play." Russ stepped up to take his turn. He got a strike, and Liam gave him a high five.

"Watch and learn." Liam moved with a dancer's grace. Brandon swore he could almost see the swish of Liam's fluffy fox tail as he lined up his approach and executed the release like a martial arts kata. His aim held true, matching Russ's strike. Liam pirouetted, took a bow to imaginary applause, and swaggered back to his seat.

"Ignore them," Justin, the sea-plane pilot, told Riley. "Before we took up poker, we had our own bowling league. Played a lot for a while, then drifted away. But muscle memory is real."

"I'm just glad we're not playing for money," Brandon said. "I suck at this."

Riley met his eyes with an impish grin. "You say that like it's a bad thing," he said under his breath so the others didn't hear.

Distracted, Brandon threw a gutter ball and endured light-hearted teasing from the rest of the crew.

Drew knocked down three pins while Noah took out six.

"Your turn." Liam looked up from his seat as the scorekeeper and nodded to Riley. "Show us what you've got."

"I played a lot in college, but that was years ago," Riley said.

"We're only playing for a round of drinks, and as one of our two guests of honor, your drinks are paid for anyhow, so low stakes," Drew reminded him.

Riley bowled a spare, which allowed him to maintain his dignity, and the others cheered.

"It's been a while since we've been to the Arcade," Noah said. "I forgot how much fun it is."

The Arcade re-used a defunct big box store in Blue Mountain Lake to offer a one-stop entertainment complex with food, a bar, bowling, arcade games, laser tag, escape room, and mini-golf. At one point, the poker group had been regulars, but they had gradually fallen out of the habit. Now, Brandon had the chance to introduce Riley to the experience.

"That's why it's perfect for a bachelor party," Russ replied.

"I'm glad I thought of it," Liam practically trilled with a joking air of satisfaction.

"Laugh it up—but I'm the undisputed master of mini-golf," Drew announced.

"In your dreams, wolf-boy," Noah joked. Drew flipped him the bird.

"Wait 'til we get to laser tag," Justin teased. "I'll show you all who's boss."

"Yeah, yeah. Keep telling yourself that," Drew razzed.

When Russ announced that they were whisking Brandon and Riley off to The Arcade for a bachelor party, Brandon hadn't been sure how that would go. But after several hours switching from one diversion to another, ribbing each other and competing for bragging rights, he decided it was a genius idea.

Russ had set up the whole thing, including a party package that offered discounted drinks and an ample spread of bar food—Buffalo wings, egg rolls, meatballs, fried zucchini, and onion rings, as well as plenty of veggies and dip. Alcohol didn't affect shifters like it did non-shifters, so only Justin and Riley needed to keep count of their drinks.

Brandon felt a rush of gratitude for their little found family, the poker gang. They had taken him in when he first came to Fox Hollow, added Noah when he and Drew got together, and now welcomed Riley.

They were Brandon's inner circle, even closer than Madden's gang at the comics store, and he appreciated having so many wonderful friends, especially after earlier times when he doubted that would ever be possible.

They each bowled their last frame, and Liam tallied the results. "Russ is in first place, two points ahead of me. Then Drew, Riley, Noah, and Brandon. Nice game, everyone."

"What's your specialty, Riley? Pinball wizard?" Russ asked as they headed toward the space-themed, black-light indoor mini-golf area.

"More of a Skee-Ball sorcerer, actually," Riley replied. "I also spent a lot of quarters and my wasted youth on two-person shooter video games and multi-player racing."

"Now you're speaking my language," Russ said with a wolfy grin. "Challenge accepted."

Liam elbowed him in the ribs. "You can't demolish one of the guests of honor at his party," he teased. "At least wait until next time."

"Oh, all right," Russ sighed in a mock put-upon tone. "But that definitely means a rematch in the near future."

"How about you?" Riley looked to Brandon as if he realized that he didn't know this detail about his fiancé.

"I'm one of those annoying people who doesn't care about the score." Brandon shrugged. "I just like being here with everyone, and I play to have fun. I'm mediocre at the games at best, terrible in general, but I don't care because I'm having a good time."

"That's why Brandon is the referee," Liam said.

Drew dominated at mini-golf, as he predicted. Brandon managed to sink enough balls not to end up with an embarrassing score. Riley scored in the middle of the group without seeming to be taking the competition too seriously.

"Having fun?" Brandon slipped up beside Riley and slipped an arm around his waist.

"Definitely. How about you?"

Brandon nodded. "I used to love this kind of thing in college. We had a place that had a huge arcade of older games and served pizza and beer. They had a theater that played black-and-white monster movies. We could go on a Saturday morning and stay all day without going broke."

"I had a friend in high school who had a video game system, and we used to play all weekend. His mom would buy us all the Hot Pockets, chips, and cookies we could eat. She would also make sure he had one of the hot new games, even though they weren't flush for cash. I used to wonder why, and I realized later she knew exactly where we were, who we were with, and what we were doing—and we were happy as clams," Riley replied. "Smart lady."

They saved the escape room for last, which was a series of five rooms, each more difficult than the last. The rooms had different themes—Haunted Mansion, Miner Forty-Niner Cabin and Mine, Sea Base Gamma One, Castle Dungeon, and Urban Explorer.

"I love these," Noah said as they queued up. "When I was a kid, I used to turn our basement into a spooky maze every Halloween for my friends."

"My parents did a scary maze in our backyard for trick-or-treat, and you had to get through it to get candy," Liam added. "They did have a 'chicken entrance' for kids who were too scared to do it."

"I had a job in college at one of those 'haunted attractions' that open up at a theme park that's closed for the winter," Brandon confessed.

Riley gave him a quizzical look. "Do tell. What did you dress up as? I've been to those. Some of them are really scary," he said.

"I was tall so I got to be Frankenstein's Monster." Brandon was sure he'd be teased about this forever now that he admitted the truth.

"That's really cool," Justin said. "I went to one of those places on vacation at the beach with a bunch of friends in high school—that scared the bejeebers out of us. It was definitely not 'family friendly.'"

"You'd be surprised how often someone jumps out at a guest and gets decked because they panic," Brandon said. "And it's always the petite teenage girl you wouldn't think could pack a punch. Saw one wipe out a guy in a ghillie suit who jumped out from the bushes on a trail. She knocked him cold—and I bet she was only about fifteen. Of course she was totally mortified. Damn, she had a right hook!"

Russ and Drew shared a look. "We used to explore abandoned buildings when we were teenagers. Not that we ever told our mom. Probably got exposed to asbestos and all kinds of gross stuff, but that was part of the charm," Russ said. "Kinda amazed we survived, now that I look back. Some of those places were a lot more dangerous than we realized at the time."

"You mean like the old paint factory with the big vats?" Drew chimed in.

"And the little defunct amusement park where we waded through the Tunnel of Love and climbed up the roller coaster track," Russ added. "Good times."

"What about you?" Liam looked at Riley. "What's your Halloween story?"

Riley's ears went pink. "I needed money my senior year in college. My dad cut me off, and I was afraid I wouldn't be able to finish. I was over twenty-one, so a friend got me a job waiting tables in a gay bar. For Halloween, we all had to dress up and work in costume. The theme was *The Rocky Horror Picture Show*."

"One of my favorite movies," Liam said. "Which character were you?"

Riley blushed scarlet. "I was the youngest person on staff and since I was a college kid, I was in pretty good shape. So I had to be Rocky."

The others cheered and catcalled as Brandon pulled him in for a kiss. "You have hidden depths," he said.

"Pretty sure you've been as deep as you can get," Riley whispered, which made Brandon's cheeks flame.

They picked two of the scenarios—Haunted Mansion and Castle

Dungeon. The group was used to working together, so tackling the puzzle meant dividing tasks and sharing information.

Haunted Mansion had hidden doors, a moving bookshelf, and a talking bust of Edgar Allan Poe that gave clues. Liam found the final piece of the puzzle and saved the day. For the Castle Dungeon, the room featured suits of armor, a talking painting, and the holographic ghost of a knight who gave unreliable information. Justin put the last clues together to get them out just before the "executioner" came to lead them to the gallows.

"Wow—that was intense," Drew said when they walked out, laughing and holding the candid photos they bought.

Last on the list was a visit to a bar themed to look like a Prohibition speakeasy. To get in, someone had to make a "call" from an old-fashioned phone booth to a secret number. A bouncer opened a hidden door and gave them plastic fedora hats, candy cigars, and elastic bow ties, then led them to a Roaring Twenties-themed bar.

"I love this," Riley told Brandon as they walked into a room where patrons mingled with costumed actors dressed as mobsters, gun molls, gamblers, and flappers. On stage, a woman in a slinky gown sang torch songs accompanied by a man in a tuxedo playing a grand piano. A huge mirrored backbar loomed behind the mahogany bar, tended by a man with honest-to-god garters holding up his shirtsleeves.

"It's pretty cool," Brandon agreed as Drew led the way to the bar. The menu offered cocktails that were trendy in the years of Eliot Ness and Al Capone, like a Gin Rickey, Old Fashioned, and Highball.

Russ was the designated driver, and with his shifter metabolism, anything he had to drink earlier was already burned off. The others ordered and found a table where they could watch as costumed actors played out short skits among the customers. Feds confronted gangsters, a flapper accused her rich boyfriend of cheating, and an informant squealed to the cops on a bookie.

"The drinks are good, and it's fun to be part of the show," Liam said. Brandon knew the fox had a weakness for anything theatrical.

Brandon held Riley's hand under the table and pressed their knees together. Their friends joked and laughed, enjoying the entertainment and swapping lines from their favorite gangster movies.

"Thanks for a great night," he told the others, and Riley echoed the sentiment. "I think this has been the most amazing bachelor party in the history of bachelor parties."

"And no one had to get covered with cake jumping out of one," Riley added.

Liam gave him the side-eye. "I came out once. Don't need to do it again."

The night was cold and clear when they piled into Russ's SUV for the drive home. Snow flurries twinkled in the moonlight, but the roads were clear and dry.

"We either need to do this more often just because or get Justin married off for a good excuse," Drew said.

"Hey, find me Mr. Right, and I'm all for it," Justin agreed. "I never expected to be the spinster of the group."

"Don't worry—your time will come." Noah patted him on the shoulder and sounded slightly sloshed.

"Kitty can't hold his liquor," Drew teased. Noah curled his fingers like claws and made a half-hearted hiss, then broke out laughing.

"Gods, what did I drink?" Noah leaned against Drew. "I never get tipsy."

"I think you passed 'tipsy' a while back." Liam arched an eyebrow. "Just don't barf on my boots."

Brandon watched them joke like brothers and felt lucky to have his found family and his fated mate. He stole a kiss from Riley, who looked pleasantly buzzed and likely to fall asleep.

"Did you have fun?" he asked in a voice just above a whisper.

"Lots. Can we get married now? I'm tired."

Brandon laughed. "Very soon. You've got time to rest up."

Riley shifted in his seat to be even closer to Brandon. "Good. This was awesome. Wake me when we get home."

THE WEEK between the bachelor party and the wedding flew past. Every day brought a list of important items to confirm and details to check.

"I can't believe there's so much to do, and we aren't having a complicated wedding." Riley fielded a phone call from the hotel's catering manager as Brandon confirmed the time with the photographer.

"Food, venue, cake, photographer, clothes, officiant, license, rings, honeymoon." He counted off on his fingers. "The hotel is doing the food, and they had deals on the cake and photographer. We've got the rest lined up."

"Do you mind not wearing tuxes? Those dress shoes are so slick on dry ground I hate to think what they'd be like on ice."

"Not at all. If we ever want to pretend to be high rollers or fancy gentlemen, we can always rent them some other time," Riley assured him.

A trip to Lake Placid's ski shops had netted them Norwegian sweaters with black and white detailed Nordic designs, a splurge they could wear often during Fox Hollow's long winters. Over black pants with black Timberlands, they could look classy and still not wipe out in the parking lot.

"It was great that Russ and Drew volunteered to take the presents back to their place afterward so we could leave directly for the honeymoon," Brandon said. "Gives us something to look forward to when we get back. We can throw a little bash for 'opening day' and have the gang over."

Brandon drew Riley in for a quick kiss. "Stop stressing. It will all be wonderful because it's *our* wedding. We're already mates—this is just another layer."

"I know, and you're right. I just want to throw a good wedding party for our friends since they're coming out to celebrate with us."

"As long as the bar is running and the food is good, they'll be happy," Brandon told him. "Everything else is icing on the cake."

"Speaking of the cake…I think Jack is going to outdo himself," Riley said. "He was really excited about the order."

"If his cake is half as good as his donuts, it'll be the best dessert I've ever eaten," Brandon agreed.

They had chosen to keep the ceremony simple, so there was no wedding party. Still, Russ and Liam threw a rehearsal dinner at their house the night before the ceremony. The poker gang was there, along with Madden and the rest of Riley's friends from the comics store.

The shifters in their friend group had gone for a run in their fur while Elias and Riley hung out and watched a movie. They welcomed their friends and partners back, snow-covered and panting, and then they all braved a dip in the steaming hot tub to warm up before dinner.

Russ grilled hamburgers and veggie burgers, and they feasted on baked beans, coleslaw, pasta salad, and a fresh vegetable medley. Jack brought donuts. Afterward, they hung out and played video games, a way to ratchet down the stress before the big day.

Now, the time had nearly come for the ceremony, and despite all Brandon's efforts to keep Riley calm, his own stomach felt tight with stress.

"I'm nervous." Brandon fidgeted with his sleeves.

"You look amazing." Riley gave him a proprietary pat on the shoulders.

"We could elope," Brandon added hopefully.

"Not with the storms coming our way. But we can spend the whole honeymoon snowed in," Riley answered, flashing a lascivious grin.

Riley's tattoo of a small moose peeked from beneath the sleeve on his left wrist, a bookend to Brandon's tat of a musical note in the same place. They had gotten the tats done the day after Brandon proposed as a reminder of their commitment.

"You have the rings?" Brandon felt a twinge of panic and patted his pockets.

"Yep. Right here." Riley took Brandon's hand and slipped it into the front pocket of his pants, letting him feel both the ring case and his half-hard dick.

"Get a room, you two," Madden said as he walked by, the unofficial master of ceremonies checking to make sure everything was going well.

What might be the last storm of the winter hung in the offing. That validated their sensible dress code of good sweaters and practical shoes.

"Looks like a full house." Brandon peeked into the ballroom at the

Fox Hollow Hotel from the service hallway door. "Seems like everyone came."

"Of course they did," Riley teased. "Madden was in charge of invitations."

"Ready to do this?" Patricia Carnes, the Fox Hollow Justice of the Peace, asked. They had already signed the licenses, so they were legally married as well as officially mated, but the brief ceremony offered a chance to celebrate their union with their friends, something that mattered to both Brandon and Riley.

In the spirit of keeping things simple and not wanting to hurt anyone's feelings, they had opted out of having any "best men," so Riley and Brandon were the only ones beside Patricia involved in the actual ceremony.

"Born ready." Riley took Brandon's hand.

"Then let's go," Patricia said. "The sooner you're married, the faster we can eat!"

They followed her from the service door into the ballroom, and everyone stood and clapped at their entrance. Brandon felt his ears go pink and Riley took his hand, giving him a reassuring squeeze.

"Please take your seats," Patricia said, and the crowd quieted and sat down. Brandon and Riley stood at the front of the room with Patricia in between.

"Brandon Davis, do you take Riley Henderson to be your mate, your partner, and your companion for the rest of your days?"

Brandon met Riley's eyes, and while he still couldn't hear his thoughts, Riley's love blasted through loud and clear. "I do."

Riley's hand shook as he slipped the ring on Brandon's finger, and Brandon closed his hand around Riley's in confirmation and reassurance.

"Riley Henderson, do you take Brandon Davis to be your mate, your partner, and your companion for the rest of your days?"

Riley looked at Brandon as if he were concentrating, trying to push his emotions, if not his thoughts, across their mate bond. "I do."

"By the authority vested in me from the State of New York, I pronounce you wedded husbands. Kiss each other and let's party," Patricia declared.

Brandon pulled Riley in for a not-completely chaste kiss, parting with goofy grins and sparkling eyes as their friends clicked silverware against their goblets.

Brandon and Riley had compiled a playlist of their favorites for the DJ, ranging from dining music to slow dances and fast songs designed to get everyone on the dance floor. He started off with mellow pop favorites while the guests lined up for the buffet.

"I hope the food suits everyone," Riley fretted quietly to Brandon.

"We reviewed the choices. There's something for every preference, and nobody's relatives are on the menu."

The hotel was well aware of the shifters among its clientele and had very strict food policies. The buffet had beef and chicken for the carnivores and omnivores, a plentiful spread of vegetables for the herbivores, and appetizers ranging from nuts to smoked salmon and sushi for those with particular tastes.

Russ, Liam, Drew, Noah, and Justin from Brandon's poker group gathered around to offer their congratulations, quickly followed by Madden, Elias, Jack, and Mico.

"We don't have to wait for someone to get married to go back to The Arcade," Russ said, referring to where they had held the bachelor party.

"That would be a lot of fun—whenever Brandon isn't taking greenhorns into the great outdoors," Riley joked.

Brandon's tours were filling up rapidly as the weather cleared. That helped, since he and Riley had decided to add on to their garage to shelter the Pilot and upgraded the couch after an enthusiastic makeout session broke the frame.

Just about everyone they knew was present. Brandon stood next to Riley with their arms around each other's waists, and Brandon felt warm and loved.

"Best wishes," Dr. Jeffries said, shaking their hands. "I hear through the grapevine that the Relocation Team has been of help."

Since Fox Hollow was a haven, many newcomers had fled their original homes under short notice. The Relocation Team helped newcomers find jobs and housing and get a foothold in the community. Riley appreciated their help in landing him a job at the music store, which was excited to have him offer lessons and work as a sales consultant. That left plenty of time for his evening gigs at the hotel, and for the requests to play for private functions which had picked up as well.

"They were great helping me get all the technical parts of moving taken care of and connecting me with the people at the store," Riley replied. "Thank you so much for your help."

"We're glad to have you in Fox Hollow," Jeffries said. "And I'm waiting to hear about the extension for the research grant, but I think it'll go through. You're going to be busy."

He walked toward the buffet, leaving Riley and Brandon alone for a few minutes.

"You have the lodge confirmation?" Riley asked.

Brandon patted his jacket. "In the inside pocket. Can't wait to sneak off with you."

They had made reservations for a week at the famous Whiteface Lodge, known for its excellent food, beautiful views, and amazing hospitality. Since it was still outside tourist season, the rates were relatively reasonable for a week's worth of pampering.

Friends had sent early wedding presents that included gift cards for the lodge's spa as well as bottles of wine and champagne. If they ever chose to leave the resort, there would be plenty to explore in nearby Lake Placid.

Brandon found that once the ceremony was over, his appetite returned with a vengeance, but he worried that Riley hadn't eaten much despite the excellent food.

"Are you feeling okay?" he murmured as guests began drifting back to the serving table for desserts.

Riley nodded. "Just a little overwhelmed—in a good way. I never eat much when I'm nervous. Took me forever to be able to eat before performing."

Brandon took his hand under the table. "Gotta keep up your strength. I've got a lot of 'aerobic' activities planned."

"I like the sound of that."

Brandon couldn't believe how much his life had changed in just a few months. From questioning whether he would ever find his "forever person" to meeting his fated mate, everything had turned upside-down in a very good way.

"Penny for your thoughts." Riley tugged Brandon toward the dance floor as a favorite slow song started. Brandon took him into his arms and held him close, swaying to the music as a slow song started.

Brandon nuzzled near Riley's ear. "Just happy. Grateful. Blessed. And a little gobsmacked that it all worked out. You?"

"All those things. I was running away from something when I came to Fox Hollow. I never dreamed I was running toward you." Riley stretched up and kissed him.

"I thought I was treading water, marking time," Brandon confessed. "I had started to lose hope. And then you showed up. Best grocery run I ever made."

All around them, their friends clinked silverware against their goblets to call for a kiss. Brandon drew Riley closer, slow and sweet, putting on a good show for their audience.

Through their mate bond, he could feel Riley's happiness, contentment—and a fair amount of lust. They were definitely on the same page. Brandon knew that he might never be able to read Riley the way his telepathy allowed with other people, but thanks to their bond, he found he was okay with that.

"The night's still young," he murmured to Riley, brushing his lips against Riley's sensitive ear. "We've got memories to make."

ACKNOWLEDGMENTS

It's always so much fun to return to Fox Hollow! Thanks so much to my cover artist, Adrijus, and to my editor, Ann Wicker, my personal assistants and promotional partners, as well as to my wonderful beta and ARC readers, and of course to Larry Martin for all his help editing, formatting, and continuity checking, among many other, very essential, things! Oh, and to Dax and Kipp, the bestest puppies, for their support.

Stay tuned—there will be more Fox Hollow books coming, as well as more in all the series. Enjoy!

ABOUT THE AUTHOR

Morgan Brice is the romance pen name of bestselling author Gail Z. Martin. Morgan writes urban fantasy male/male paranormal romance, with plenty of action, adventure, and supernatural thrills to go with the happily ever after.

Gail writes epic fantasy and urban fantasy, and together with co-author hubby Larry N. Martin, steampunk and comedic horror, all of which have less romance and more explosions.

On the rare occasions Morgan isn't writing, she's either reading, cooking, or spoiling two very pampered dogs.

Watch for additional new series from Morgan Brice and more books in the Witchbane, Badlands, Treasure Trail, Kings of the Mountain, Sharps & Springfield, and Fox Hollow universes coming soon!

Where to find me, and how to stay in touch

Join my Worlds of Morgan Brice Facebook Group and get in on all the behind-the-scenes fun! My free reader group is the first to see cover reveals, learn tidbits about works-in-progress, have fun with exclusive contests and giveaways, find out about in-person get-togethers, and more! It's also where I find my beta readers, ARC readers, and launch team! Come join the party! https://www.Facebook.com/groups/WorldsOfMorganBrice

Find me on the web at https://morganbrice.com. You can also find me on Twitter/X: @MorganBriceBook, on Pinterest (for Morgan and Gail): pinterest.com/Gzmartin, on Instagram as MorganBriceAuthor, on YouTube at https://www.youtube.com/c/GailZMartinAuthor/ on Bookbub https://www.bookbub.com/authors/morgan-brice and on TikTok @MorganBriceAuthor

Check out the ongoing, online convention ConTinual www.facebook.com/groups/ConTinual

Support Indie Authors

When you support independent authors, you help influence what kind of books you'll see and what types of stories will be available because the authors themselves decide what to write, not a big publishing conglomerate. Independent authors are local creators supporting their families with the books they produce. Thank you for supporting independent authors and small press fiction!

ALSO BY MORGAN BRICE

Badlands Series

Badlands

Restless Nights, a Badlands Short Story

Lucky Town, a Badlands Novella

The Rising

Cover Me, a Badlands Short Story

Loose Ends

Leap of Faith, A Badlands/Witchbane Novella

Night, a Badlands Short Story

No Surrender

Warm You Up, a Badlands Short Story

Point Blank

Memory and Malice, a Badlands Novella

Shine Tonight, a Badlands Short Story

Fox Hollow Zodiac Series

Huntsman

Again

Silent Partner

Fox Hollow Universe

Romp

Nutty for You

Imaginary Lover

Haven

Gruff

Trash and Treasure

www.ingramcontent.com/pod-product-compliance
Lightning Source LLC
Chambersburg PA
CBHW020637110726